Ghost

The Perished Riders MC - Book 4

Nicola Jane

Copyright © 2022 by Nicola Jane.

All rights reserved.

No portion of this book may be reproduced in any form without written permission from the publisher or author, except as permitted by U.K. copyright law.

Meet the Team

Cover Designer: Charli Childs, Cosmic Letterz Design
Editor: Rebecca Vazquez, Dark Syde Books
Proofreader: Jackie Ziegler
Formatting: Nicola Miller

Disclaimer:
This book is a work of fiction. The names, characters, places, and incidents are all products of the author's imagination and are not to be construed as real. Any similarities are entirely coincidental.

Ghost can be read as a standalone, but it is the fourth book in The Perished Riders MC and therefore would make more sense if read as part of the series.

Spelling Note

Please note, this author resides in the United Kingdom and is using British English. Therefore, some words may be viewed as incorrect or spelled incorrectly, however, they are not.

Acknowledgements

To Paul, for always loving me so hard and for allowing me to love you back. xx

And to my boys, who make me proud every day and are the reason I keep going. xx

Contents

TRIGGER WARNING	IX
PLAYLIST	X
CHAPTER ONE	1
CHAPTER TWO	14
CHAPTER THREE	27
CHAPTER FOUR	41
CHAPTER FIVE	56
CHAPTER SIX	69
CHAPTER SEVEN	85
CHAPTER EIGHT	100
CHAPTER NINE	113
CHAPTER TEN	122
CHAPTER ELEVEN	136
CHAPTER TWELVE	147
CHAPTER THIRTEEN	158
CHAPTER FOURTEEN	171
CHAPTER FIFTEEN	186

CHAPTER SIXTEEN	198
CHAPTER SEVENTEEN	210
CHAPTER EIGHTEEN	222
CHAPTER NINETEEN	231
CHAPTER TWENTY	242
Dice - The Perished Riders MC	252
A note from me to you	264
Popular books by Niocola Jane	266

TRIGGER WARNING

The material in this book may be viewed as offensive to some readers, including graphic language, sexual situations, murder, violence, and sexual assault (however, the author does not go into detail).

And remember, this is an MC romance, it is based around a fictional world of a Motorcycle brotherhood created in my head. It will not suit everyone and I do not expect you all to love it, but no part of this story should be compared to 'normal' life.

These characters make bad choices, use terribly offensive language and are often involved in drama. If you're after a sweet romance, you're in the wrong book. However, if you want a story that tugs at your heart while making you yell at your Kindle, then step inside, Ghost is waiting for you...

PLAYLIST

Go - Cat Burns
Fingers Crossed - Lauren Spencer-Smith
Whiskey On You - Nate Smith
A Little Bit Yours - JP Saxe
Losing You - James Arthur
Block me out - Gracie Abrams
Give Me The Reason - James Bay
All For You - Cian Ducrot
Flowers - Lauren Spencer-Smith
lie to me - Tate McRae ft. Ali Gatie
Can't Never Could - Savannah Dexter ft. Jelly Roll
Hate That I Love You - Jonathan RoyFallin' - Jessica Mauboy

CHAPTER ONE

NELLY

"I need help," I tell Rylee, flopping onto the couch beside the President's ol' lady.

She closes the book she's reading and turns sideways to face me. "Okay, who am I killing?" she asks, her expression serious. I smile. She doesn't even know what I need, yet she's happy to help. We've been friends for a couple of years, ever since I helped her leave her abusive ex-husband with the help of The Perished Riders MC.

"You can keep your knife in its case," I joke. "It's not that kind of help. My parents are in London for a few weeks sorting out some business, and I need to show them I have my life together here."

Rylee frowns. "Don't you have your life together?" I scoff. "Yes, did I forget to introduce you to my wealthy husband who owns a beautiful house in Sandringham?"

"Nelly, they're your parents, why do they care if you're single? Being in a relationship doesn't mean you have your life together."

I roll my eyes. "You don't know them." I sigh, feeling like a bitch. "They mean well and they're great, honestly, but they think I'm settled with a good job and a wonderful fiancé."

"You've lied to them already?"

I nod, shame washing over me. "Mum was always setting me up on dates, and I got sick of it. When I met my ex, she backed off, so I didn't tell her we'd split up."

"So, you want a fake boyfriend?" she asks, laughing.

"I know, it sounds crazy, but it's just for a few weeks. Then they'll go home, and I probably won't see them again for another six months."

"I don't know any men who your parents might approve of," says Rylee. "We could ask Arthur if he knows someone. Or maybe one of his brothers could help you out?"

I screw my face up in a way that tells her I'm not a fan of that idea. Arthur Taylor and his brothers are big time London gangsters. If I ask them for a favour, I'll have to repay them, and Lord only knows what they'd want from me. "I was kind of thinking of one of the guys here," I suggest, looking around the mc club.

"You want a biker to pretend to be decent?" she jokes. She looks around the clubhouse too before shrugging. "Okay, well, just go ask someone."

"They're more likely to do it if the Pres's ol' lady was to ask." I smile sweetly, and she groans. "Please, I wouldn't ask if I wasn't desperate. It's a couple of dinner dates at most. I'll even pay."

"I guess free food might entice them." Rylee looks around again. It's always busy in the evenings, which is why I love this shift the best. I've been working the bar at the clubhouse for a few years, ever since I pushed my way in here and convinced Maverick he needed me. It was supposed to be temporary to help me out with cash after my relationship broke down. But I love it so much, I can't face leaving. "What about Michael?"

"The vicar?" I almost screech, and a few of the guys look our way. I lower my voice. "I can't ask a man of the church to lie for me."

"Good point. Dice?" I shake my head. "No, he stresses me out with his weird behaviour and the way he rolls the dice to make every damn decision. I can't imagine my parents would be impressed with him rolling sixes to decide what dinner he wants."

Rylee laughs. "Tatts or Ghost then?"

I consider the pros and cons quickly in my head. "Tatts," I decide. He's a typical guy who never seems to have a girlfriend and prefers drinking with his brothers over dating. I think my parents could overlook the tattoos, and Mum would fall for his cheeky laddish banter.

Rylee shouts him over. "We need your help."

He eyes us suspiciously. "Is it gonna get me hurt by the Pres?"

"It's more for Nelly than me," Rylee explains. "She needs a date."

His eyes fall to me, and he narrows them suspiciously. "You wanna date me?"

"Not for real. It's an act to get my parents off my back. They're in town for a few weeks, so it'll be a three-week max kind of deal."

He screws his nose up. "I don't really do parents. The last girl I dated took me to meet her olds and they moved to another country two days later, taking her with them. I'm not the sort of man that dads like their daughters to date."

"Can't you just act for a couple of nights?" asks Rylee.

"It depends. What do I get out of it?"

"The knowledge you helped Nelly out of a tight spot."

Maverick joins us, placing a kiss on Rylee's head. They're so sweet together, I find myself watching them closely with envy. They give singletons like me couple goals that I'll probably never achieve. "What's going on?" he asks.

"Nelly wants a fake boyfriend for a couple dates over the next few weeks," Rylee explains. "I'm trying to convince Tatts that he would make the ideal man for the job."

Mav sniggers. "You know he scares parents to move their daughters to other countries. You'd be better with someone responsible, like Ghost."

"Yes, Ghost. He's way better at charming people," agrees Tatts before making his escape.

I glance over to where Ghost is sipping his bottle of beer. Out of all the guys, we don't speak much. I get the impression he doesn't like me, and he scowls an awful lot whenever I try to make conversation with him. Rylee waves him over, but he hesitates before joining us. "We need your help," says Rylee. "Nelly needs someone to pretend to date her for the next few weeks."

"No," he says firmly before walking away again.

"Brother," snaps Mav, and Ghost groans before returning and forcing a tight smile for his President. "Don't disrespect my ol' lady like that," he warns.

"Sorry, Pres. I didn't mean to. I just don't wanna get involved in whatever girl drama this is," he explains.

"She just needs someone to accompany her to a few dinners," says Rylee.

"It's fine. Don't worry about it, I'll sort it myself," I mutter, feeling my face burn with embarrassment. I didn't want to make such a big thing about it, and now I feel like everyone is listening in.

"What the fuck else are you gonna do?" Mav asks Ghost. "You're not on any jobs for me, so you're free."

"I just don't wanna pretend to date Nelly," Ghost snaps.

"Yah know, your attitude lately is shit. First, you disrespect my ol' lady by walking away when she's still talking to you, and now you're snapping at me?"

"Honestly, it's fine. It's not a big deal," I mutter.

"Nelly looks after us. She pulls all the hours she can, and she needs the club's help," Mav continues like I haven't spoken. "So, why won't you help her out?"

Ghost looks irritated. "Is it a club problem?"

"It is now, I'm making it club business. Make yourself free for whenever Nelly needs you. Is that clear?" asks Mav.

"Crystal, Pres," mutters Ghost through gritted teeth.

Mav grins and stands, pulling Rylee with him. "Great. We'll leave you to discuss the details. Nelly, if he messes up, tell me." They walk away hand in hand, and I sit awkwardly, hoping the ground will swallow me whole.

"I'm really sorry, Ghost. I wanted Tatts to do it. Let's just forget all about it. I'll tell Mav I sorted it."

He scoffs. "I'm the second choice?"

My face burns. "No. Mav said you'd be better at it."

"He's right. Don't choose a boy to be a man. And that's what you want, right? A man to show your parents you're doing good in life?" He looks amused, and I feel like he's laughing at me. "What lies do you need me to spout?"

I knot my fingers together the way I always do when I'm embarrassed or nervous. I don't know why I feel like this when usually I'd tell him to fuck himself. "There's a dinner at my uncle's house tomorrow. I'll introduce you to my parents there. We won't stay for dinner. I'll get us out of it. Just an appearance will be fine."

He shakes his head. "Nuh-uh. If you've got me embroiled in this, we're going all the way. I've got a quick thing with Star," he says, checking his watch. "I'll be back before you finish your shift at eleven." He heads for the stairs, and I watch after him. How does he know when my shift ends?

GHOST

I bury my nose into Star's hair, pushing deeper into her. She fists the sheets, groaning with pleasure. Out of all the club girls, she's the one I have the best time with. And lately, seeing everyone around me settling down has me visiting her way more than I should. Since Mav returned as President, he's had this aim to get the brothers to settle down. He wants the club to feel like a family again, and apparently, filling the place with ol' ladies and kids is the way forward.

I get it. Back in the day, even with his dad, Eagle, as leader, it felt good to be part of the club. Mav, Grim, Scar, and I grew up together in the club, and now that we're patched members, we want that tradition to continue. Except I don't ever meet that one woman who can hold my attention. Women these days are worse than men when it comes to hooking up, and then trying to find someone who tolerates the club life over everything else, just makes my search harder.

I close my eyes, moving slow and deep while picturing Harriett. She was a another one that got away. After the club helped her escape her abusive husband, we got close, though not close enough for my liking. But she was never ready for more, and now, she's moved on from the club to start her life again. She wants friendship, and who can blame her after everything she's been through.

I grip a handful of Star's hair and speed up, slamming hard against her arse and chasing the release I so badly need. Her pussy clenches my cock, and she cries out, shuddering beneath me and soaking the bed sheets with her orgasm. I feel the warmth, and it sends me spiralling with her, growling as I empty into the condom. "Fuck," I mutter, dropping down beside her. She gives me a sexy grin and tucks herself into my side.

"Did anyone ever tell you, you're hot?" she asks, placing gentle kisses over my chest.

I tangle my fingers through her hair. "I gotta go," I whisper, feeling her body sag with disappointment. "Pres has me doing Nelly a favour," I add. "I need to speak to her before she leaves."

"What kind of favour?" Star asks, running her fingers over one of the many tattoos I have on my arm.

"Club business," I say, sitting up. I remove the condom and knot it before grabbing a tissue to wrap it up. I pull up my jeans and stuff it in my pocket. I don't wanna get caught out by a club girl—give them a full condom and a pin and I'll have an unwanted ol' lady with a kid I never asked for. "I'll check in tomorrow."

"Maybe I'll be busy," she mutters, wrapping her sheet around her naked body. I shrug. She's trying to get a reaction, but she knows I don't share, so if she goes to another brother, I won't visit her again. That's the deal we made.

I head back to my room where I dispose of the condom and take a shower. I get downstairs at exactly eleven, and Nelly is just pulling on her coat. I don't know much about her. The other brothers love her, but I don't see the fascination. Sure, she's pretty and maybe a little curvier than I'd usually go for, but she's always made it clear she's not the kind of girl you can mess around with. And these days, she's good friends with all the ol' ladies, so you upset one, you upset them all, and that's not a situation a brother needs to be in.

I hold up my bike keys. "I'll take you home." She blushes. I've never seen it before, but every time I've spoken to her tonight, she's reacted the same. I never had her down for shy.

Outside, I throw my leg over my bike and pass her the spare helmet. She puts it on and climbs on behind me. Her hands go to the sissy bar and, for some reason, I place my hands behind each of her knees and tug her closer until she's practically flush against me. She automatically grabs my kutte to steady herself, and I pull her arms to encircle my waist. Something about having her cling to me feels good, like it's natural. I guess we need to act that way if we're gonna lie to her parents about us.

NELLY

All I can think about the whole ride back to my house is how much I want to grind myself against Ghost. I go on the back of the guys' bikes all the time, since they often drive me home if I get off work after ten, but I've never felt this kind of heat. Being close to him has awoken something inside of me that none of the other brothers has before. Maybe it's the fact he's never bothered with me. He doesn't ever try it on with me or flirt like some of the other single brothers.

When we stop and I climb off to hand him the helmet, my legs are weak and I'm practically panting. With a shaky hand, I pull out my keys and lead the way up the garden path to my rented house.

It's small, but I love having my own space. Mav has offered for me to move into the clubhouse more than once, but I'm not ready to give this up.

I turn on the lights as we pass through the living room and head into the kitchen. "Don't you like the dark?" asks Ghost, smirking.

"Not really," I admit, and his smirk fades when he sees I'm serious. "I once got locked in a cupboard, and since then, I've hated the dark."

He takes a seat at the breakfast bar as I shrug out of my coat. "Nice place."

"Thanks. Look, about tomorrow, I really want to just make a quick appearance to welcome my parents back and then I'll tell them we already have plans for dinner."

"Why are you lying to them?" he asks.

I pull two beers from the fridge and pass him one. "They worry about me. A lot. They're happily married, and they want the same for me. Mum sets me up on dates whenever I'm single."

"What's wrong with that?"

"The men she chooses don't want someone like me," I mutter, embarrassed at having to explain it.

"What's that mean?"

I pluck at my jumper like that explains it. "They want eye candy on their arm." I'm more Netflix and cuddle, not wine bar and socialise. I know women who spend hours getting tans, nails, eyebrows, and lashes, but I'm not that sort of girl. And rich men don't want to take me to galas and lavish functions.

And that's alright with me, but it's the sort of man my parents envision me with.

"I'm not gonna give you compliments," he states, and I laugh. "It's not what Mav hired me for."

"I wasn't fishing. I'm just saying that I'm not high maintenance and the men mum sets me up with are looking for that."

"Let's go over what you expect from me," he says, taking a pull from his beer.

"Just go with it. They never met my ex in person, so they don't know anything other than we were engaged."

He almost chokes on the beer. "Engaged?"

I nod. "Yeah. I kind of told them we'd taken the next step because they were getting itchy feet. We'd been together two years before we split up, and I never told them we'd split."

"Your lie is getting out of hand, Nelly. Why don't you just explain you're not together."

"You don't know what they're like," I mutter. "And I'm in too deep now. They're here a few weeks on business and then they'll go home. I won't see them again for months. I can come up with a whole dumping story by then."

"You're not close then?"

I lower my eyes and begin knotting my fingers again. "I just disappoint them a lot."

"Fine. Don't go all puppy eyes on me. I'll do what you need but expect me to pull in a favour of my own occasionally."

I nod, smiling. "Deal."

CHAPTER TWO

GHOST

I'm tired and short tempered. I always get like this when I don't sleep, which is pretty often. It doesn't help that in church earlier today, my brothers bet cash that I wouldn't see this shit with Nelly through. According to them, I'm too set in my ways after being single for so long, they think I can't hack the commitment. They're wrong. There's one hundred quid riding on this, and I can't wait to take it from them.

When I go down to the bar at six to meet Nelly, ready for her family gathering, she eyes me with a disapproving stare. I want to storm off to my room and tell her to forget the entire bullshit thing, but Mav is at the bar too, smirking as he watches the pair of us. "You need to lose the kutte," she says, gently.

"No. I never take this off, and I'm not about to now."

"Come on, Ghost. You think her parents will be impressed she's dating a biker?" asks Grim.

"I don't give a shit," I snap. "If she don't like me the way I am, forget it."

"I didn't say that," mutters Nelly, pulling that sad expression again, and I groan.

"I can't lie," Mav says, grinning, "I'm enjoying this. I can't wait to see how it plays out."

"You know, since you cleaned this club up, you've had too much time on your hands," I say, shrugging out of my kutte and handing it to Star. "You should get out more instead of using me for your entertainment."

We step out into the car park, and Nelly pulls out a set of car keys, handing them to me and leading the way over to a shiny BMW. "I rented it," she explains. "It looks better than arriving on the back of a bike."

I bite my tongue, snatching the keys and getting into the car. She gets in beside me and pulls down the interior mirror. "I've put the address in the SAT NAV," she says as she opens her purse and begins applying makeup.

"I feel like your damn chauffeur," I mutter, starting the engine and pulling out into traffic.

We arrive at the address twenty minutes later. The house is stunning, and as we slowly drive up the winding driveway, it takes my breath away. It's like the types of houses you see in movies about millionaires, with lights illuminating the front steps and large white pillars either side of the super-sized doorway.

I'm so entranced by the house, I don't notice Nelly's perfectly made-up face or the way her curls fall over her shoulders since she removed her hair clip until I open her passenger door and she steps out under a glowing garden lamp. I stare for a few seconds before gathering myself and hooking out my arm for her to take. "Let's get this out the way so I can get back to Star."

"Are you and she a thing?" Nelly asks, letting me lead her up the stone steps.

"Bikers and club girls are never a thing. She looks after me until I find an ol' lady to do the same job."

Nelly scrunches up her nose in disgust. "Nasty," she mutters as the large door opens and a man dressed in a black and white suit welcomes us inside. "Showtime," she adds.

We're shown through to a large room with bookshelves from floor to ceiling. There are a few people talking in low voices, and as we enter, they fall silent, all eyes on us. An older man with grey hair steps over, holding out his hand for me to shake, which I do. "Welcome. I'm Alex, Nelly's uncle." He then kisses Nelly lightly on the cheek. "Good to see you, Nells."

"My goodness, look at you," gushes a blonde lady rushing towards us. "You look radiant."

"Mother," Nelly says, smiling fondly as the lady wraps her in a hug. "This is . . ." She pauses, frowning, and her mum glances between us, waiting for a name.

I smile awkwardly and hold out my hand. "Eric."

"Eric?" Her mum looks at Nelly, confused. "I thought he was called—"

"No, Mum, he's always been Eric," Nelly says sharply. "His middle name is Rob, and he sometimes goes by that," she lies. "Let's stick with Eric. Where's Dad?"

"Eric, it's lovely to finally meet you. I'm Charlotte, and my husband, Adam, is—" She looks around before smiling.

"Right here, darling." Nelly's dad appears behind his wife and kisses her on the cheek before offering me his hand. "Adam. Pleased to meet you."

"Same."

"I'm amazed you're finally meeting us after all this time," Charlotte goes on to say. "You're always so busy. Nelly tells us you love working in law?"

Nelly gently squeezes my hand, and I force myself to nod, but I don't back my answer with words in case she sees through my lie. I wasn't prepared, and Nelly is to blame for that. She must feel my annoyance because she quickly changes the subject. "Anyway, we can't stay. I told you we have dinner plans, but maybe we can meet for lunch next week?"

"Nonsense," says Adam. "We haven't seen you in months, darling. Have dinner with us."

"Really, we can't," says Nelly.

I squeeze her hand and smile wide. "This is more important than dinner with friends, *darling*. Let's stay and eat with your family."

Nelly glares at me, and I smirk. "It would be rude to cancel our plans so near to the time," she grits out through clenched teeth.

"Surprise, I cancelled them earlier because I knew how much you wanted to have dinner with your parents," I say.

"See, we like this," says Adam, patting me on the back. "Let me get you a drink." I let him lead me away, leaving Nelly with her mum.

Nelly's family is bigger than she let on, and Adam takes me around the room to introduce me to various cousins, aunts, and uncles. When we're eventually seated in a ridiculously large dining room, I'm placed between Nelly and her cousin, Nova.

Starters are placed before us by wait staff with ninja skills who seem to just appear out of nowhere. I stare at the pâté. I've never eaten a posh meal in my life, but as I spread it on my cracker, I decide one night of luxury might be nice.

"I can't believe you did me like that," Nelly whispers.

I grin. "A man needs food."

"I would have gotten you a takeout," she hisses.

"And miss this," I say, holding up half the cracker before popping it in my mouth. "You forgot to tell me I was a lawyer called Rob. No wonder you left your ex. I bet he was boring as fuck."

"Actually, he was nice . . . when he was sober."

"I have a drinking problem too?" I ask, fake gasping. "Then fill me up," I add, grabbing my glass of beer.

Nelly places her hand on my forearm, preventing me from drinking. "He also used to hurt me when he was drunk. Are you gonna go that far while in character?" she snaps.

I lower the beer, feeling like a dick. "Sorry."

"Let's just get through this the best we can and forget the whole thing. It was a bad idea. I'll make an excuse for any other events they insist we go to."

But it's not as easy as that, and later, when Adam insists we go to his business associate's birthday party, I end up agreeing on Nelly's behalf.

Once dinner is over, we say our goodbyes, and Adam hands me a card with the details for the event. Nelly eyes me suspiciously, and the second we get outside, she turns on me. "What the hell was that?"

"Erm, I kind of agreed to go to some guy's birthday bash. It's at a swanky joint in central London. I think you'll love it."

Nelly pinches the bridge of her nose. "I won't. We can't go."

I pull her to a stop, and she glares up at me. "Look, you should spend time with your parents while they're here, especially if you're not going to see them for a few months. I'll be on my best behaviour."

She groans. "What if someone asks you about law?"

"I've spent my life blagging. And I know a lot about the law, mainly how to break it, but I'll put a spin on it."

"I think you're right—this is getting out of hand. I have to come clean." She turns back towards the house, but I stop her, taking her wrist and pulling her back.

"One more and then we can make excuses. Don't upset your parents over something so stupid. One day, you'll meet a guy and can show him off for real, but until then, I don't mind being your stand-in." I can't let her give up on the first date. Mav and the guys would never let me forget it.

NELLY

Ghost stops outside my place. "Thanks for helping me out," I tell him as I get out the car. I'm surprised when he follows me. Once inside, I turn to him, expecting him to leave, but when he passes me to go to the kitchen, I frown. I don't know where this sudden keenness has appeared from, when earlier, he couldn't stand me. Now, it's like he can't be apart from me, even arranging more family get-togethers. I watch him go through the fridge, pulling out some out-of-date items and throwing them in the bin. "When did you last shop?"

"Haven't you got somewhere to be? Isn't Star wondering where you're at?"

He shrugs. "Probably. I thought we could get to know each other better seeing as we've got to keep this act up and your family were so much more nosier than you said they'd be. Your cousin, Nova, was extremely suspicious."

"She was probably wondering why you were with me."

He looks at me over the fridge door. "What do you mean?"

"Well, look at you," I mutter, pulling my jacket off, "and look at me. Nova is the princess of the family. She spends a fortune to look that amazing, and the men she attracts are like you but with less tattoos."

"I never realised you had such low self-esteem," Ghost points out, closing the fridge with a beer in his hand. "You're almost out of beer."

"I don't drink it often, so it's not a problem."

"Why's it in your fridge?"

I feel my cheeks flush as I shrug. "For guests."

Ghost arches a brow, smirking. "Male guests?"

"For the record, I don't have low self-esteem. I just recognise I'm not on the grade-A list of hot women, but I'm okay with that. Besides, I have a good personality."

"Yet to be seen," he mutters.

He follows me to the living room, and we sit on opposite couches. "Where did we supposedly meet?"

"Ghost, they're not gonna ask that. Why would they care?"

"I'm asking the questions, you answer them."

I sigh heavily. "A party. You were in town for business. You later moved here to be with me. Although, I soon realised that wasn't the case, and you just needed a place to stay and an easy lay while you made your name in London."

He grins. "And have I made my name?"

"Rob is a grade-A, first class wanker. He thinks he's big in London, but he isn't. His personality, notoriety, and cock size are all way smaller than he will admit."

"Me and this guy are worlds apart," says Ghost, taking a pull of his beer. "What did you mean earlier when you said he wasn't very nice to you?" I twist my fingers, and his eyes fall to them. "Why do you do that when you don't wanna talk about something?"

I pull my fingers apart and place my hands under my thighs. "He liked to drink. Had a problem with it. He was nasty with words. He'd put me down and rip into me."

"Small cock and a bad personality. How long did you say you stayed together?"

"Two years. It's been over a long time. In fact, I recently bumped into a nicer ex, so maybe I'll be able to introduce my parents to a real boyfriend soon." I leave out the part that he already knows my parents very well.

"You should be careful seeing other men while you're embroiled in this lie, Nelly. What if your parents see you out with this guy?"

"Why haven't you settled down? What are you, thirty-something?"

"It would be unfair for me to keep all this love for one woman," he jokes, and I roll my eyes. He shrugs, staring down at his bottle. "I just haven't met that one who makes it all stop. I thought I had, with Harriett, but she's not ready, and I'm not sure she ever will be."

"It's a shame. I thought you guys were cute together."

"I'm happy that she's happy. I'd probably only break her heart. I'm good at fucking shit up."

"Me and you both," I agree. "Yah know what's good for self-pity? Vodka!" I go to grab my emergency bottle.

I peel my eyes open and groan when the light penetrates my brain. The room spins as it comes into focus. "Nelly," hisses Ghost, "wake up, your parents are downstairs."

I sit up too fast and slam my hand over my mouth to try and deter the impending need to vomit. "Huh?"

Ghost is standing in my bedroom door, glaring at me. "Something about breakfast?"

I shake my head, refusing to speak or get out of bed. I flop back down. "No," I whisper desperately.

"Why on earth are you still in bed?" Mum's voice comes from the hallway, and then she appears in the doorway next to Ghost. "Are you sick?"

I nod but Ghost laughs. "No, she's hungover. Get up, Nelly, we're going for breakfast."

I scowl as he moves closer, hovering over my bed with a stupid grin on his handsome face. "You grassed me up," I croak, and he laughs again, then takes my arms and pulls me to sit up.

"Get dressed."

Blue Garden is a posh place my parents love to eat at, so I'm not surprised when I'm instructed to meet them there. I dress and head downstairs to find Ghost sipping coffee. He slides a bottle of water towards me. "I told you vodka was a bad idea," he says.

"But you still drank it with me."

"I can handle it," he says dryly. "I had to put you to bed when you started singing Madonna at two in the morning."

I snigger and down some of the water. "I can handle breakfast. You get on with your day."

"I already told your parents I have the day off, so I said I'd be there. Besides, they want me to meet their business partner."

I choke on the water, spilling it down my chin. "Hugo?" I spit out. "Let's skip breakfast. I can't face them today."

Ghost shakes his head. "Not a chance. We're going."

"Why are you so keen on this all of a sudden?"

"I never quit a mission." He holds up the car keys and winks. "Besides, you almost choked at the mention of Hugo, so of course I need to see what that's all about."

We're led to our table where my parents both stand to greet us. Seconds after we sit, Hugo arrives, greeting my parents, and then Dad turns to us. "Hugo, meet Nelly's fiancé, Eric."

Hugo sniggers as they shake hands. Then, he leans down to kiss me on the cheek, lingering a little longer than he needs to. Taking the seat on my left, he shrugs out of his expensive suit jacket, and when his arm brushes my own, I shiver. Dad and Hugo get stuck in conversation about business and profit margins. Mum begins to grill Ghost on his life, and I hold my head in my hands, willing my brain to stop pounding.

"You're very quiet, Nelly," says Hugo.

I glance up. "Headache," I mutter.

"Hangover," Mum corrects.

"I know a great cure. Follow me," says Hugo, taking my arm and pulling me to stand. Ghost frowns but remains quiet as Hugo leads me over to the bar, where he orders a bottle of water. He pulls out a tablet and drops it in the bottle, then gives it a shake. "Thought you'd broken things off with your boyfriend," he snaps.

"Long story," I reply, taking the water and drinking some.

"I'm coming over tonight, so you can explain then."

"You shouldn't. It's not a good idea." Secretly, I'm thrilled I have his attention. There's twenty years between us, but when I'm with Hugo, I feel so alive. The only catch is, he's my dad's best friend and business partner.

CHAPTER THREE

GHOST

I don't like Hugo. I knew the second his lips lingered for too long on Nelly's cheek that I didn't like him. And now, as I watch the way he leans in to talk to her at the bar, I want to smash his smug face in. He doesn't know I'm not her damn fiancé, so he's disrespecting me. When they return to the table, Nelly's cheeks are flushed and she's smiling like she holds the answers to all the secrets in the world.

We get through breakfast exchanging light conversation, and after we've eaten and everyone stands to say goodbye, I grab Nelly's hand. It surprises us both, but I don't let go until we're back at the car and she pulls free. "You're fucking a man old enough to be your dad," I snap accusingly. It was plainly obvious by the way she blushed whenever he looked her direction and the way they kept 'accidentally' brushing arms.

Her eyes widen but I know I'm right. She hesitates too long to make her next lie believable. "No."

"Bullshit. He's your dad's business partner, Nelly. What the hell are you thinking?"

"Christ, you met my dad less than twenty-four hours ago and now you're watching his back?" she snaps, getting in the car. I lean in and pull the seat belt across her, clipping it into place.

"If you don't want me to know, I suggest you stop making fuck me eyes at him." I slam the door and march around to my side, getting in and slamming that door too.

"I was not," she hisses, her cheeks flushing red.

"And giggling like a fucking child at all his jokes. They weren't even funny."

"I'm not talking about this with you, Ghost. It's private business, so stay out of it."

"Why don't you just come clean and tell your parents you have a thing for their friend. That way, you can stop lying."

"It's complicated," I mutter.

"Yeah, by twenty-plus years."

She checks her watch. "Take me to the club. I have to start work in half an hour."

"Yes, ma' lady," I say, my voice dripping with sarcasm.

I head straight into church when we get back to the club, and all eyes are on me as we sit down. "What?"

Mav smirks. "You stepped out last night?"

"Before you get any stupid ideas, nothing happened between Nelly and me, and it won't. We drank vodka, and I crashed."

Grim slaps me on the back. "That's how it starts."

"N-next th-thing you know, she's in y-your b-bed," Scar, my blood brother, adds with a laugh.

"I'm not like you guys," I snap. "I don't like Nelly like that. I just wanna win this fucking bet so you all realise I'm not avoiding relationships. I'm choosing to be single."

"Keep telling yourself that," says Tatts.

Mav clears his throat, and we all settle down to discuss the week's business. Things in the club are running well and we're turning over a good profit without doing too much criminal work. Rylee has also opened a women's centre just up the road from the clubhouse. There's support in place there for those who need help with debt guidance, job advice, and domestic abuse help.

"Rylee is going to ask Nelly if she'd like a role at the centre," Mav informs us. "It's about time we got her more involved in the club. She's proved to be a great employee and she's loyal."

"And now she's dating Ghost," Copper throws in, and the other brothers laugh.

"Shut the fuck up," I mutter.

"Ghost, check on Harriett today. We've not heard from her this week," Mav instructs, and I nod. We check in on the women we've helped on a weekly basis.

Church is called to an end, and I head for the bar so I can apologise to Nelly for snapping at her. She's right, it's her business, and I shouldn't judge. Star steps in my path and places her hand over my chest. "I waited up for you," she whispers. "You didn't come." She hands me my kutte.

"I had business," I explain, slipping it on. It smells of her perfume.

"I'm free now if you have time," she says, biting her lower lip. My eyes flick to Nelly, who's laughing at something Rylee is saying. Star's hand goes to my already semi-hard cock. "Take that as a yes." She stands on her tiptoes and presses her lips to mine. I keep my eyes on Nelly—why the fuck can't I look away? Star rubs my cock until it's straining against my jeans. Nelly looks over and her smile falters as I pick Star up and she wraps her legs around me. Carrying her towards the stairs, I try to wipe the feeling of guilt from my mind as I take her to my room.

Harriett looks pleased to see me when I enter her little boutique. "Stranger," she greets, rushing over and kissing me on each cheek. Posh women always go for two kisses.

"How are you?"

"I'm good. Busy with this place. Trying to juggle childcare is a nightmare."

"You know, there's a place for you at the club. The ol' ladies can help with all that stuff."

"And, like I keep telling you, I'm happy living above this place." With the settlement money Harriett received from the breakdown of her marriage, she bought this shop and the apartment above it. She now runs this popular kids' clothing boutique. "What's going on with you?"

I take a seat on the velvet chair near the counter. "Not a lot. Mav's got me helping Nelly out. I think he likes to keep me busy with pointless shit."

"Is she okay?"

I nod. "She lied to her parents about having a fiancé and they're in town, so guess who got the part."

Harriett laughs. "Oh, wow. How's that working out?"

"Fine. We only went on one date, two if you count breakfast today. Her parents seem okay. I don't know why she doesn't come clean cos I don't think they'd care." I shrug.

"She always felt like she was disappointing them," says Harriett. A customer hands over some garments, and Harriett sets about de-tagging them and ringing them up on the cash register. "She wasn't comfortable in their world."

"What does that even mean?"

"Thanks, have a good day," she tells the customer. "Money. They have a lot of it, and they go to the fancy parties and charity balls to keep up the appearance. She hates all that."

"She told you that?"

"Yeah. I get that world. I never felt comfortable in it either, so I got what she meant."

"If her parents have so much money, why does she work behind the bar at the club?" I ask. She hesitates, so I know she knows. "Tell me," I demand.

"I think she had a fling with someone at their company. His wife found out and threatened to tell her parents if she didn't leave."

I frown. "So, she walked out of a good job?"

Harriett nods. "Yes, she couldn't stand to upset her parents and disappoint them, so she moved to London."

"This man, from the company, was he older?"

Harriett shrugs. "Not sure, she didn't say, but she really liked him. He broke her heart. After him, she ended up on a downward spiral and it took her a while to get her shit together again."

NELLY

"You have to come," Meli begs.

"I really can't. I have plans," I explain, pulling my coat on.

"If you change your mind, we'll be at Dice's bar." I nod, knowing the place. It's another bar owned by the club, and the ol' ladies love it there.

I get home and rush to shower, then I pull on skinny jeans and a low-cut vest. I curl my hair and apply a small amount of makeup to hide the dark circles under my eyes. Checking my watch, I realise I have ten minutes to spare. I smile as I pour a glass of white wine to settle my nerves. It's been years since I was alone with Hugo, and I can't deny I'm excited.

Time ticks by. He's twenty minutes late, but I soothe myself by pouring a second glass of wine and putting some music on. Business often runs over, and he's here in London to meet with new contacts, so maybe he went for a quick drink.

An hour passes and I check my mobile for the hundredth time. No message. No missed call. I try calling him again, but it goes to voicemail. I slam my phone down. What did I expect? This is Hugo all over—empty promises. Fuck waiting around for him. I'm over that, so I grab my coat and head out.

By the time I get to Dice's bar, the girls are tipsy like me, and they throw their arms around me in excitement. It makes me feel slightly better as I take a glass of wine from Rosey. "I can't believe you came," says Meli.

"Plans changed," I mutter.

"Did they involve a man?" she asks, grinning.

"An old flame. No one important. We were supposed to be catching up."

"Not the guy who was horrible to you?" gasps Rylee.

I shake my head. "No." I want to add that Hugo was so much worse for my heart than Rob ever was.

"How was your date with Ghost?" asks Rosey.

I smirk. "You mean Eric?" We all laugh. We're so used to the guys using their road names, it seems foreign when we hear their birth names. "It was fine. My parents didn't say anything negative about him, so that's got to be a good sign."

"When you think about it, it's kind of sweet he's agreed to do this," says Hadley.

"Mav forced him," I point out. "Before this, he hated me. Maybe he still does."

"That's impossible," says Rylee, hooking her arm into mine and leading me to the bar. "You're too nice to be disliked."

It's great to catch up with the girls. The club is so busy these days and everyone has a role in one of the businesses, so we don't get to see each other as much as we once did. When it's closing time at the bar, Rosey and Meli drag us all back to the clubhouse so we can continue the party.

Ghost is watching a football match on the big screen with Scar and Dice. He side-eyes us as we pile into the club. Meli turns on the music, and Rosey grabs a bottle of vodka from behind the bar. Mav comes out of his office, and Rylee throws herself at him. "An after party," he says, grinning as Rylee kisses him. "I told the guys it needed to be a quiet one tonight, maybe I should have warned you ladies."

"How often do we do this?" Meli complains. "Let us live a little."

"It is Friday," adds Hadley.

"I guess I can make an exception this once," Mav replies, tapping Rylee's arse as she heads back to us.

My mobile lights up and I stare at Hugo's name. "Gonna answer that?" comes Ghost's voice from behind me. I jump in fright and shove the phone in my bag. He sits beside me as we watch the women dancing to Spice Girls. "What should I wear to the party tomorrow?"

"I've already told you, we aren't going."

"Because Hugo will be there?" I detect amusement in his voice. "Why's a guy like him single?" He stares at me, waiting for a response, and when I don't bite, he grins. "He is single, right?"

"Why are you so interested, Ghost?"

"Because we're a pretend couple, so I have a right to know who you have sex with."

"Stay out of my business."

"You're making me look like an idiot," he says. "He thinks we're together for real and then you're flirting with him."

"Are you being serious?" I snap.

"He's no good for you, and you can do better."

"You know nothing about it."

"I know he's married."

We glare at each other, and after a few long, silent seconds, I sigh. "He's not happy in his marriage."

Ghost laughs hard, throwing his head back and wiping his eyes. "Oh dear God, tell me you didn't fall into his bed because he spun you some shit about not being happy. Did he tell you he sleeps on the couch too?" I sit straighter, refusing to embroil myself in his jokes. "He did, didn't he? He told you that and you fell for it? Nelly, come on, I thought you had a little common sense."

My phone buzzes in my bag, and when I see Hugo's name again, I head out front to answer. "I am so sorry, Nells" is the first thing he says. "I got stuck at a meeting."

"Don't worry."

"I feel really bad. I had a whole reunion planned. I was gonna get us takeout and bring wine. I wanted to make it special. I even got you a gift."

"Hugo, honestly, it's fine. I made other plans anyway."

"With your boyfriend?"

"No, my friends. I have to go." I disconnect, and when I turn to go back inside, Ghost is there holding his keys.

"Mav's broke up the party cos they woke one of the kids. Do you want a ride home?"

Ghost pulls the bike to a stop outside my place and we both get off. "Thanks," I say, handing him the spare helmet.

"I'll walk you inside." I lead the way up the garden path and into the house. "Did your parents find out about Hugo?" he asks as he helps me remove my jacket. "Is that why you left?"

I shake my head. "No. They don't know, and they'll never find out so long as I stay away."

"What did you do . . . at the family business?"

"It's not important. It's all in the past."

"I bet it was better than working behind a bar in a biker club."

There's a knock at the door and we fall silent, staring at each other like one of us should know who's behind the door. Eventually, Ghost marches over and pulls it open. "You've got to be shitting me," he mutters. "A fucking booty call?" he snaps, glaring at me, while Hugo stands awkwardly in the doorway. "You're a fucking idiot, Nelly." Ghost pushes past him and leaves.

"Bad time?" asks Hugo, stepping inside and closing the door.

"What are you doing here?"

"I came to see if you were okay." He holds up a bottle of wine, but I can see he's already had a couple. "I got us wine."

"You're a few hours too late."

He hands me the bottle and begins to remove his coat. "What's wrong with lover boy?"

"Do you honestly think if he was my boyfriend, he'd have walked off and let you come inside?" I ask as he follows me into the kitchen. "He's my friend . . . sort of. I needed to get my parents off my back."

I grab two glasses, and Hugo steps closer, running a hand over my shoulder. I close my eyes and shudder. I've missed his touch. "God, I miss you, Nelly," he whispers. "So much."

"How's Karen?" I ask, placing the glasses on the counter.

"Don't," he mutters, turning me to face him. "Let's just have one night how it used to be."

"When you'd pay for hotels by the hour," I say bitterly.

"I think we both know we spent more than an hour together."

"But never a whole night."

He runs his fingers along my jaw. "It's easier to move on when I don't see you, but the second you walked into the restaurant this morning, it hit me like a tonne of bricks."

"We can't do this again, Hugo," I murmur.

"One night," he whispers, moving his lips a breath away from my own. "We can have one night." He pauses, giving me the chance to stop him, right before he kisses me. I melt against him, gripping his shirt in my hands and pulling him closer. It's been so long since anyone kissed me like this, and I feel like he's lit a spark inside me.

Within seconds, we're ripping at each other's clothes, tugging, pulling, panting, desperately trying to free the parts we need. He lifts me onto the counter, gently pushing me to lie back, and then he tugs my jeans down my legs. He hooks one over his shoulder and kisses the inside of my thigh, working his mouth up towards the one place where I ache for him. When his tongue licks my opening, I almost buck off the counter, gripping my fingers into his hair.

I come quickly, grinding against his mouth and writhing around like a born-again virgin. When he stands and produces a condom, I want to cry in relief because I need this man. I need everything he can offer.

GHOST

"What shift is Nelly on?" I ask Mav.

He glances at a rota beside his desk. "She should be here any minute. Everything okay?"

"Perfect," I mutter, heading to the bar to wait. When she finally arrives wearing sunglasses and a grim expression, I waste no time annoying her. "Good night?"

"Yep."

"Was it a late one?"

"What do you want, Ghost?"

"Did you fuck him?"

She rips her sunglasses off and narrows her eyes. "Did you fuck Star?"

"Yes, but she isn't married. Jesus, Nelly, he's got grey hair."

"Some women like a mature man, a silver fox."

I scoff. "More like a scraggy dog."

"Why do you care so much?"

"Because he's one of the reasons you're so down on yourself, don't you see that? You let him use you and then you feel degraded and not good enough."

"Or I feel sexy and satisfied."

"Until the next morning, when he returns to the wife he's never going to leave. Just do me a favour . . . avoid the old married guy and look for someone who will treat you right. You deserve it, Nelly."

CHAPTER FOUR

NELLY

I rush home after my shift at the bar to change for the stupid party Ghost agreed to. I try calling Hugo, but he doesn't pick up, so I send a message telling him I enjoyed last night and asking if he'll be at the party tonight. And if I'm honest with myself, that's the only reason I'm going, in the hope Hugo will be there. Being with him last night was like old times, like we'd never been apart. He's got this way of making me feel safe and needed. I was disappointed when he'd left this morning before I'd woken up, but I know he'll have a good reason.

When Ghost arrives at seven to pick me up, I'm glad to see he's driving a car and not his bike. I take in his suit and smile. He looks good, and his tattoos poking out over his white collar add to the sexiness he's got going on. "Well look at you," he says, taking my hand and holding it above my head while I spin slowly to show off my long red dress.

"I thought I'd make the effort," I tell him, grabbing my matching bag.

"There's something hot about a woman dressed in red. Especially red lipstick," he says, eyeing my lips with a heated expression. I feel myself blushing. If only a guy like Ghost would look at me in that kinda way for real.

We arrive at the hotel, where the party is just getting started. There are already hundreds of people filling the room, but I spot my parents chatting with Hugo by the bar, so I tug Ghost towards them. We do the usual greetings, and as Hugo kisses my cheek, his hand caresses my arse. I bite my lip to hide my smile, but I can't help the fluttering I get in my stomach every time we do this flirty thing in public. As I pull away, Ghost wraps his arm around me and tugs me closer into his side. I glance at him, confused, but he continues speaking with my mum. More people arrive at the bar, pushing us into a tighter circle, and Hugo is so close, I'm sandwiched between him and Ghost.

Hugo hooks his little finger around mine and asks, "Can I get you both a drink?"

Ghost holds out his hand. "Sorry, Hugo, I forgot to say hello." Hugo takes his hand, and Ghost pulls him close and leans into his ear. "Take your hands off my fiancée now or I'll break your fingers."

I gasp, and Hugo smirks. "Got it. He's taking his role very seriously," he adds, amused, as he releases me and steps to the bar.

"Ghost," I hiss.

"I'm doing you a favour, baby. You'll thank me for it later."

"When I'm in bed alone?" I snap.

He grins, placing a finger under my chin and tipping my head back. "If it's a hook-up you're looking for, there are better guys than him. Trust me." I stare at his lips, and he smiles wider. "Naughty girl," he whispers, placing a chaste kiss on my nose. I frown, confused by his odd behaviour as he goes back to chatting with my parents like he didn't just flirt.

Hugo hands me a glass of wine, and I take it gratefully. "You look amazing," he says quietly, not wanting to attract Ghost's attention.

"You left early," I say.

"Work," he answers. "I have a room booked here this evening, number three-five-zero."

I blush. "I'm not sure I can get away."

"From your fake fiancé?" he asks, smirking.

"It's rude to come with him and then dump him."

He gently moves the hair from my shoulder. "I'll make it worth your while," he whispers, giving me his sexy, smouldering eyes. Those damn butterflies take flight in my stomach again. "I need to spend every waking moment buried inside of you, Nelly. I can't stop thinking about you."

I smile. "I'll do my best."

"So, Hugo, you work for Charlotte and Adam?" asks Ghost, bringing everyone's attention to us.

Hugo smiles tightly. "With, not for," he says. "What do you do again?"

"Law," says Ghost. "And you're married, kids?" he adds.

"Married, two kids," he mutters.

My heart squeezes. Two kids? Last time we hooked up, he had no kids, and now in the space of a few years, he has two? "How old?" I ask, my voice breaking slightly.

"Two and one."

"Wow. You left it late," jokes Ghost, and my parents join him in laughing.

"Well, my wife is a lot younger than myself."

"Really? You like them younger then?" asks Ghost.

"I need the bathroom," I mutter, placing my drink on a nearby table and rushing off.

I shove the bathroom door harder than I mean to and it crashes back against the wall. Gripping the sink, I stare at myself in the large, brightly lit mirror. "Fuck, fuck, fuck," I whisper.

The door opens and Hugo stares at me. "I was going to tell you," he blurts out.

One of the toilets flush and a female steps out. She gives me an awkward smile, washes her hands, then rushes out. "When, exactly?"

"It doesn't change anything. I've missed you and I'm here in London for the next few weeks. Let's make the most of our time together. I can stay at yours."

I shake my head. "It's not a good idea."

He moves closer, gripping my upper arms. "Nelly, come on, you know you've missed me too. I feel it. I feel the spark we have, and I know you do." His mouth crashes against mine in a clumsy, desperate kiss as he pushes me up against the wall. I allow myself to get carried away and revel in the feel of his hands roaming my body. When we pull apart, he smiles. "Tonight," he confirms, and then he leaves.

Ghost eyes me suspiciously when I return. "Everything okay?" he asks.

"Uh-huh."

"Your lips are swollen."

"Don't start," I hiss.

"Just imagine having that same rush you get kissing him but with a man who thinks the world of you," says Ghost.

"Why are you giving me relationship advice? When was your last girlfriend?"

"I don't have relationships, Nelly. If I did, I'd be him," he snaps, pointing to Hugo, who is schmoozing a group of men. "I'd be that guy who left his beautiful wife and kids at home and fucked a desperate whore on the side. All men want to have their cake and eat it. It's just some guys have morals and then some don't, like me and your friend, Hugo."

"So now I'm a desperate whore?" I hiss.

"You're sleeping with a married man, you tell me." He walks away and disappears into the crowd. A stray tear slips down my cheek and I brush it away angrily. How dare he judge me when he sleeps with club girls.

It's an hour before Ghost finds me propping up the champagne bar. I hate the stuff, but it's free. "I have to go. Can I drop you home?" I shake my head. "Look, sorry about what I said. I just want you to see you're worth more."

"By calling me a whore?"

"Do you want a ride or not?"

"No. You get back to your club whore. I'll stay here with the free champagne."

"Harriett called. I'm not rushing off to sleep with Star."

I knock the rest of my glass back. "Whatever. I don't care."

"Are you staying for him?" he asks. I lower my eyes, and he nods angrily. "Fine."

"Are you leaving?" Mum asks, approaching us.

"Yes. I have a thing," says Ghost before he turns to me. "I'll call you tomorrow, baby," he says kindly. There's an awkward silence where neither of us knows what to do because Mum is still here and couples don't just wave goodbye. Ghost takes a deep breath and gently touches my cheek. We stare at each other, both dreading what's about to come. "I love you," he says, the words sounding foreign. He leans close, his lips brushing mine, and I suck in a surprised breath. I thought his kiss would be hard and rough, but his lips are soft. He must feel intrigued too because instead of pulling away, he kisses me again. His other hand cups my cheek and he angles my face for a better kiss. I instinctively open my mouth and then we're full-on kissing.

GHOST

I've kissed a lot of women, but none have ever gotten my cock hard like Nelly. The way her mouth fits against my own and the way her body pushes against me makes me wanna scoop her up and take her back to my bed, caveman style.

When we eventually pull away for air, we're both stunned. I use my thumbs to clear the red lipstick from the edges of her swollen lips before wiping my own mouth on the back of my hand. The spell we seem to be under is broken when Hugo calls Nelly's name. "Nelly, there's someone I want you to meet." She blinks a few times, and I release her. "Nelly, come over here."

"You should go. The old guy is calling you," I mutter, stepping back. I watch her go to him like there's some sort of invisible force pulling her away from me.

Fuck, what the hell just happened?

Harriett is waiting on her doorstep with Ivy asleep in her arms. "Thank god," she cries. "It's huge."

I grin, wiggling my eyebrows suggestively. "You've never even seen it," I joke, and she narrows her eyes. "Okay, okay, show me the enormous spider."

We head inside to her bedroom and she points to the corner where a sizable spider is clinging to the wall. I roll my eyes. "Really?"

"That's big, Ghost, even you have to see I couldn't suck that in the vacuum." I scoop the innocent beast into my hands and take it outside, releasing it into the garden. Once Harriett has taken Ivy to bed, she joins me downstairs. "I'm sorry I interrupted your night. Coffee?"

Harriett doesn't drink and she doesn't have any alcohol in her house. Understandable seeing as her ex-husband was a big drinker. "Sure."

"What were you doing? I don't think I've ever seen you in a suit."

"Helping Nelly out. It was a guy's birthday party in some flashy hotel."

"Oh god, I'm so sorry. Why didn't you say you were busy?"

"Because I wasn't. I didn't even wanna go to the party. I just . . . I'm proving a point to Mav and the guys." She hands me a coffee, and we go into the living room and sit. "Mav reckons I don't commit. He said I couldn't last pretending to be Nelly's fiancé because I'm so set in my ways and I never make room for anyone."

"Why do you care what the guys think?"

I shrug. "Maybe I want to prove it to myself too. Am I scared to settle down? Maybe I push women away on purpose."

"That's not true. You just haven't met the one yet."

"We both know I have," I mutter.

"Ghost," she says, groaning. "You know as well as I do that we're great as friends, but I'm not good in a relationship. I love having my freedom back and my independence. I don't ever see me giving that up again."

"I wouldn't ask you to."

She smiles kindly, and it makes me feel like a fucking charity case. She feels sorry for me. "Not intentionally, but you would. It's in your DNA as a biker, as a Perished Rider. Besides, I couldn't ask you to change for me."

I stand, placing my half-drunk coffee down. "I should go."

"Ghost, don't be mad. I love you as a friend."

I nod. "I know, but I can't put myself through this. I need to take a break. Get these crazy feelings under control. Then I can go back to being your friend and I can stop wanting more."

"See, the guys are wrong. You want to commit . . . I'm only sorry I don't feel the same."

I feel angry, mainly with myself for letting my mouth runaway with itself. I put my heart out there when I knew Harriett didn't feel the same, and now, I feel like shit. And I've probably made her feel like shit too. I groan aloud, and a passing couple eye me warily. I get in the car and head back to the club, needing whiskey and my brothers and maybe sex.

Scar is in the bar watching Gracie. He's always watching her. She's with the other ol' ladies in the safety of the bar, less than a metre away from him, but he still watches like he's terrified she'll disappear right before his eyes.

"Copper, get me the whole bottle," I tell my brother, who is already pouring me a glass of whiskey. He arches his eyebrows and hands me the glass and the bottle.

"W-what's wrong?" stutters Scar. It's a speech impediment he's struggled with his whole life.

"I fucked up. Twice."

"A-about time you were t-the f-fuck-up," he says, grinning. "Whatever y-you did, I'm gonna t-tell Mum and revel in my m-moment."

I laugh. "It's nothing serious, brother. I'm not as big a fuck-up as you just yet. I kind of laid my heart out there for Harriett to trample."

"Ouch."

"And I kissed Nelly."

He glares at me. "W-what?"

"I know. It just happened. Her mum was there, and I was saying goodbye. I'm supposed to be her fiancé, right, so I can't just walk out of there without some affection. I go in for a peck and somehow end up kissing her."

"W-what did she say?"

"Nothing. Some douchebag she knows pulled her attention away, and I left. The thing is . . . it wasn't terrible."

Scar smiles. "Y-you enjoyed it?"

I nod. "If that room had been empty, I'd have done a hell of a lot more than kiss her, brother."

He grins. "So, why did y-you end up at Harriett's?"

"She called to get a spider out her place." I bury my face in my hands and let out a long, loud groan.

"L-let me get this s-straight. You left Nelly to remove a s-spider?"

"Harriett needed me, and the party wasn't my thing. I was glad to get out of there."

Scar shakes his head, looking unimpressed. "Sh-she called, and you w-went running."

I laugh. "What can I say, brother, I'm a sucker for a pretty woman."

"Two p-pretty women, and y-you're here with me drinking w-whiskey?" He arches a brow.

"Good point," I mutter. "I should go and see Nelly, apologise."

Scar slaps me on the back. "M-maybe you'll w-win that bet after all."

NELLY

I wrap a sheet around myself and shuffle until I'm sitting on the edge of the bed. "Don't look at me like that," mutters Hugo as he fastens his shirt.

"Why didn't we stay in your room at the hotel?" I ask.

"I told you, it's safer here. What if your dad had called in for a nightcap?"

"Won't he wonder where you are if he does that?" Hugo sighs. He doesn't like questions, and I'm irritating him. I expect his wife never asks him anything, which is why he gets away with sleeping with other women. "Two children," I say, because I don't feel like that information has quite sunk in.

He pulls his jacket on. "Do we need to do this, Nelly? Did you expect me to never have kids? It was natural progression in my relationship with my wife." His words sting.

"The relationship you once told me was dead?"

"Things change. We changed. Look, I'm not in London for long, so do you want to spend this time together talking about my family?"

There's a knock at the door, and I frown. Who would be calling around at midnight? "I'll call you," says Hugo, leaning over and kissing me on the head. I follow him to the stairs, wrapping myself tightly in the bed sheet again. I stop halfway down as he opens the door. Ghost stands on the threshold, glaring at Hugo as he pushes past to leave, paying no attention to the angry-looking biker.

I lower until I'm sitting on the stair, and Ghost steps inside. "You fucked the old guy?"

"Don't, Ghost," I whisper, my voice breaking. A tear rolls down my cheek because I know I've been stupid. I've been used yet again.

"Don't start crying," he snaps. "You let me kiss you," he yells angrily. "You let me fucking kiss you and then you fucked the old guy."

"Stop calling him that. You went to Harriett's, so he offered to see me home."

"I would have seen you home if it meant I got an easy fuck," he shouts. I cry harder, trying to wipe the tears away before they roll down my cheeks. "I'm an idiot, thinking that kiss was something. I came here to fucking apologise for leaving you tonight. I'm a fucking idiot." He storms out, slamming the door hard behind him.

I hardly sleep, and by lunchtime the following day when I arrive at work for my afternoon shift, my eyes are sore and swollen. I keep my sunglasses on as I go behind the bar to dump my bag and coat. Rylee comes over and asks, "You okay?" I nod, because if I speak, I'll cry. "The big glasses are hiding something . . . a hangover?"

I pull the glasses off and glare at her. She gives me a sympathetic smile, and it's enough to bring on a fresh set of tears. She rushes around the bar to embrace me. "What happened?"

"I'm angry with myself," I admit. "I slept with Hugo."

"Hugo? Married ex, Hugo?"

I nod. "I don't know what I expected. He's married. Nothing's changed. Apart from the fact he's got two kids now."

"Shit."

"I'm so stupid. Why did I do it? I forgot how much it hurts to watch him leave and to have him ignore my calls. I feel like that reckless teenager who would do anything for him."

Rylee strokes my hair away from my face. "We've all been there, sweetie. Some men just have that power over us, and as much as we try and fight it, we always give in. Don't be too hard on yourself. He's the married one."

"I hate myself," I mutter. "I spent years not thinking about him, and now he's back, he's all I can think about."

"He's the one that got away. Seeing him again made your heart want what you always dreamed of."

I let out a heavy sigh. "And Ghost kissed me."

Her mouth falls open in shock. "What?"

"And I liked it."

We both grin. "Oh my god. Did he like it too?"

I groan. "That's the other thing. He came by last night, after the kiss, but it was as Hugo was leaving. He was pretty mad." I wince.

"That explains why he's storming around the place like a bear with a sore head."

I roll my eyes. "Great. I'll try and avoid him."

"Or you could just kiss him again," she suggests, winking.

CHAPTER FIVE

GHOST

"What the fuck is wrong with your attitude?" snaps Grim, glaring across the table in church.

"Sorry, VP," I mutter.

"Things not going to plan?" Mav smirks. "Should I expect the money from our bet?"

I scowl. "Put me on collections for Arthur today," I say.

"No chance are we putting you out there in your mood. We're the nice guys, remember," says Grim.

"Nice guys who force people to hand over weekly rent for a gangsta?" I ask, my voice laced with sarcasm. Collecting Arthur Taylor's protection money is the only criminal activity we're currently involved in.

"Are you trying to push my fucking buttons?" snaps Grim.

Mav shakes his head, telling Grim not to bite, and then slams the gavel on the table. "Get out of here and earn the club some money," he tells everyone.

I head for the bar with Grim close behind me. "Star, come suck Ghost off before he gets himself killed."

Star smiles, placing her hands on my chest and leaning up for a kiss. I tug on her hair and let her run kisses along my jaw. My cock doesn't move. I gently place my hand around her neck and kiss her back, but the buzz isn't there, and I growl. "Forget it," I mutter, pulling away. When I look up, Nelly is watching us. Her eyes are swollen and red like she's spent hours crying.

"Ghost, take Rylee to the gym," orders Mav. "Get a workout while you're there and burn some of that anger off."

Rylee wants to spar, so we forget the gym and head down into the club's basement. It's where the men used to go to fight, back when Eagle was in charge. She puts on the gloves, and I pick up the pads. "Why are you so angry?" she asks, tapping the pads.

"Make it worth it," I mutter, pushing her fist back hard with the pad.

She hits with a bit more force. "Mav said you were angry."

"I'm fine. Can't a guy be in a mood without getting the third degree?"

"Nelly's the same. She's feeling upset and sad today." I shrug like I don't care. "She said some guy used her. I'm tempted to send Mav to beat the shit outta him."

"You can only be used if you let someone use you."

"She's weak when it comes to this guy. She spent her late teens loving him, and he treated her like crap."

"When will she learn then?" I snap. "I know about Hugo, Rylee. I also know her last boyfriend was a shit too, so why does she keep going for dicks?"

"She listens to her heart and not her head. A lot of us women are like that. If you ask me, Hugo was the one in the wrong. He saw how vulnerable she was as a teenager, and he took full advantage. He was the married one."

"And she knew that. The guy wasn't gonna turn down sex when it was offered to him on a plate."

Rylee hits me harder. "Men are so easily swayed. It's not an excuse. If you're married, you don't fuck around."

"Decent men don't, but Nelly doesn't go for decent men."

"Decent men don't seem to find her. She's so nice. I just want her to find a guy who will look after her." She stares at me with meaning, and I shake my head.

"Don't look at me. Nelly isn't my type."

"Bullshit."

"I'm telling Mav about your bad language," I threaten.

"Nelly is gorgeous. You'd be mad not to see it."

"She's not my type," I repeat. "I like my women like I like my meat. Lean."

"Stop being an arse."

"Nelly is lying to her parents, she's sleeping with married men, and she's too curvy for me. She doesn't wear enough makeup, and the list goes on, so don't get any ideas about setting us up. I'm pretending to date her for a fucking bet, nothing else."

Rylee stares past me with her eyes wide and her mouth open. I slowly turn to where Nelly is standing holding two bottles of water. She jumps into action, forcing a smile and placing the bottles on the floor. "Mav said you'd need water." Then she turns and rushes back up the steps.

"Good one," hisses Rylee, hitting me hard in my arm.

I close my eyes briefly. "Fuck. Did she hear it all?" The worst thing about it is I didn't mean a damn thing I just said.

"Yep."

I find her a few minutes later, wiping down the bar top. She looks distracted and tired. "Nelly," I mutter, and she jumps, looking startled, "about what I said."

"I don't know what you mean," she says, smiling.

"I know you heard."

"I'm really busy. I have to get on." She heads round the bar and starts to spray the tables while I follow her.

"Just hear me out."

"No, I don't need to. You're entitled to your opinion. And what you said was true. I am lying and shagging married men, though for the record, it's one married man. I'm also curvy . . ." She frowns, taking a shaky breath. "Although I never saw it as a problem. And I'm not your type. That's okay, cos you're not mine either."

I nod. "Good. Great. No harm done then."

She goes back to wiping tables. "And thanks for helping me out with my parents. You've done more than enough. I can take it from here."

"Isn't your cousin's wedding next weekend?"

She nods. "Yes, but I'm happy to go it alone. I've got to eventually, right?" She smiles as if to convince me.

"Nelly, about the kiss—"

She holds up her hand. "Please, just leave it. It was a mistake, a show for my parents. I hope I didn't repulse you too much." She laughs nervously.

"You didn't re—"

"Good. See you around." She heads for the toilet, slamming the door and locking it.

NELLY

I take a few deep breaths, feeling so embarrassed. Of course, he doesn't like me in that way, why would he? I stare at myself in the mirror, suddenly hating my curves, when there's a light tap on the door. "Nelly, it's me," says Rylee.

I unlock the door, and she slips inside. "I am so sorry," she begins.

I wave my hand in the air. "It's fine. Honestly. It's not like I liked him or anything. I'm still hooked on Hugo . . . obviously."

"I just wanted to set you up with someone who would take care of you. I'm sure he didn't mean any of it. I think he was trying to convince himself more than me."

"Am I fat?" I ask, turning sideways to check my appearance again.

Rylee throws her arms around me. "God, no, you're not at all. He's an arse for even saying that. I'd kill for your womanly curves."

"Because I've never worried about my weight. I go to the gym, sometimes. I eat okay . . . ish."

"Nelly, stop! You are not fat. I'm gonna make Mav put him on all the shittiest of shit jobs for a month," she rages.

I smile. "Toilet cleaning duty?" I suggest.

"Yes. And babysitting duty. He hates that."

"Thanks, Rylee. For, yah know . . . being nice."

"I love you, Nells. The right guy's gonna come for you, and when he does, you'll wonder why you ever wasted time on Hugo."

The rest of my shift passes in a blur. I do everything I can to avoid Ghost, which isn't hard, seeing as he seems to be doing the same. Dice comes over, and I hand him a beer. He's not really a talker, so I go back to stocking the fridges. "I would have done it if I'd have known he'd be such a dick," says Dice.

I turn to face him again, feeling honoured to have him speak to me. "Pardon?"

"The whole date thing. I would have stepped in if I knew Ghost was gonna be such a prick. I heard what he said about you."

"It's fine," I mutter, feeling even more humiliated. *Is everyone talking about it?*

"If it helps, Mav's stuck him on clean-up for a week. He's outside now washing down the bikes, and then he's got to babysit Rosey and Meli this evening." I smile, and he chuckles. "That's better. The place ain't the same when you're not smiling, Nells." He takes his beer and walks away. My heart feels a little happier because at least Mav and the others have my back.

Later, after my shift, I'm about to leave when Ghost takes me by the hand and pulls me towards his bike. "Pres said I have to drop you home."

"I'd rather walk."

"Not an option. Get on the bike or I'll put you on it."

I'm annoyed by his cold tone, but I get on the bike and hold on to the sissy bar cos there's no way I'm touching him. When he tries to pull me closer, I shuffle back again. I spend the entire journey trying hard to keep every part of my body away from his, and that's a task on a moving bike.

Once we stop outside my place, he goes to step off, but I hold up my hand. "No. I don't need you to come inside, Ghost."

"Nelly, I just want it to go back to how it was between us. We were getting along."

"And then I heard what you really think of me. Let's just stay away from each other and make it easier on us both. Out of interest, what was the bet?"

"A hundred that I couldn't stick it out, dating you."

I nod, a sad smile pulling at my lips. "Right. I should have known." I walk away, my heart feeling heavier once again.

I shower and pop some leftovers into the oven for my dinner, then find a good film on television and settle in. My mobile shrills on the table, and it's Meli. "Get dressed in your shortest dress and put on some heels and lipstick. We're coming to get you."

"Not a good idea. I'm not good company."

"That's exactly why we're coming for you, Nelly. Rylee said you were fed up, and we never leave a woman behind. You're coming out. No excuses." She disconnects, and I stare at the blank screen. Great. A crazy night with Meli and Rosey . . . not what I need right now.

Rushing upstairs, I open my wardrobe, and staring back at me is a short black dress I'd purchased months ago but never had the courage to wear. It literally just about covers my arse. I pull it out and slip it on, running my hands over my hips as I stare at myself in the long mirror. I like it. My legs look longer, and it makes my arse look great. It's exactly what I need to forget Ghost's stupid comments cos this dress shows all my perfect curves.

I pull out my makeup bag and apply it minimally, but then his words fill my head again and I reapply darker eyeliner and extra mascara.

When the girls arrive, I'm waiting at the door with my handbag and heels. I slip them on and climb in the taxi. "Look at you," says Rosey, grinning. "Sexy lady."

"It's something I threw on," I joke. "No bodyguard?"

"They're meeting us there. Just a heads-up though, Ghost will be there and he's in the worst mood ever," says Meli, rolling her eyes. "Sometimes club punishments backfire on us."

She isn't wrong. Ghost is already waiting in the bar for us with Dice, and his face says it all. "Cheer up, Ghost," says Meli, smiling. "It could be worse . . . you could be in a room of fat women."

He rolls his eyes. "I didn't say she was—"

"Enough," I snap. "I'm here to have a good night and I don't want to be reminded of what went down earlier today. So, someone get the shots flowing and let me find a man who appreciates my fat arse." Meli and the girls break into fits of laughter as Ghost scowls angrily.

"Single ladies, show me the dance floor," says Meli, grabbing my hand and pulling me away.

We dance, laugh, and drink cocktails, and it's exactly what I needed to forget the past twenty-four hours. Meli has her eye on a group of men at the next table, and she makes no secret of it as she shakes her arse and throws them flirty smiles. One of them holds up a bottle of champagne and indicates for us to join them. Ghost grabs my wrist as I go to follow the girls over to their table.

"Not a good idea, Nelly," he warns. His mouth is close to my ear, and I shiver. I'm drunk and feeling things I shouldn't at the sound of his gravelly voice.

"It's the best idea," I say, trying to pull free from his grip.

"I'm serious, you don't even know those guys."

"Maybe I'll find another married one seeing as I love them so much," I snap.

"I thought we were over that. I apologised."

"Why do you care?" I ask, and he stares at me for a few seconds. "Why do you care who I talk to?" I ask again.

"Because I can't stop thinking about that damn kiss," he grits out angrily.

I finally pull my arm free and rub where he held. "I bet that really fucking annoys you," I snap. "Wanting to fuck the fat girl." I walk away and join the girls, who are now sitting with the men, chatting and sipping champagne. It takes me a while to relax. Deep down, Ghost's words have hit a nerve and they're playing on my mind. Every so often, my eyes drift to where he's hitting the whiskey hard.

When it's time for us to leave, Ghost can hardly stand. "Nelly, can you stay at the club tonight? It would make it easier if we didn't have to drop you home now he's in this state," Dice explains, glaring at a very drunk Ghost. "He can't drive, so we're gonna have to get a cab."

"Do you think it's a good idea for Pres to see him like this when he was supposed to be watching us?" asks Meli.

"Good point," mutters Dice.

"Look, why don't I grab a separate taxi to mine, and he can stay with me?" I suggest.

"I'm sitting right here," snaps Ghost. "Stop talking like I'm not here."

"Meli's right, brother, Mav ain't gonna let this slide. You gotta sober up at Nelly's," says Dice.

"Wow, I'm so impressed," says Meli sarcastically. "You made a decision without rolling your dice." He gives her a sarcastic laugh, rolling his eyes in annoyance.

We head out from the nightclub and flag a cab. Ghost and I take the first one. It seemed like a good idea when I suggested it, but now, sitting alone with him, I feel nervous. "Yah know, I would have been okay to go back to the club," he mutters, resting his head back. "I could have gotten on my bike. I'm fine to drive."

"You can pick your bike up tomorrow."

"Why'd yah offer to let me stay at yours when you hate me?"

I sigh. "I don't hate you."

When the cab draws to a stop, I pay the driver and Ghost follows me in, swaying and tripping behind me. Once inside, he props himself against the wall and closes his eyes. "You can take the spare room," I say, kicking off my heels and locking the front door.

We go upstairs and I show him to the extra bedroom. "Thanks for this," he mutters.

"You helped me out, so I'm returning the favour."

"The kiss—" he begins, but I close the door, leaving him in the room. I don't want to talk about the damn kiss.

I'm just sliding into bed when my door opens, and Ghost stands there in jeans that are riding low on his hips. His black boxer briefs peek over the top. I frown, wondering what the hell he could possibly want now. I try not to stare at his rippling muscles or his hard chest. And I definitely don't want to look at the tattoos covering his skin. "I can't sleep."

"You just got in there, did you even try?" I ask.

He sits on the edge of my bed. "It's weighing on my mind," he says. "The kiss."

"Jesus, Ghost. I'm tired. The kiss meant noth—" His lips crash against mine before I can finish my sentence.

"Please don't say it meant nothing," he eventually whispers against my mouth. "It meant something." I swallow hard, staring into his blue eyes. "I don't know who I was trying to kid earlier when I said all that stuff about you, Nelly, because I didn't mean a damn word of it. When I knew you'd heard everything I said, it killed me inside. I hate that I upset you cos I never want to be the one to upset you. You're perfect in every single way, and I hate that I feel like this, but fighting it isn't working for me either. I got wasted tonight because I didn't like seeing you laughing with those guys. I tried so many times to make you laugh like that and failed but they got to do it in under five minutes."

"I was fake laughing," I mutter.

"You were still laughing. The thing is, I think I want to be the one to make you laugh. I want to kiss you whenever I feel like it. I want to call you in the middle of the night when I can't sleep, just to hear your voice. I think I like you, Nelly . . . a lot more than I was supposed to."

CHAPTER SIX

GHOST

Nelly looks terrified. But it's been said now, and I can't rewind, so I kiss her again, and she lets me for a third time. If she was completely repulsed, she'd stop me, right?

Eventually, her hands grip my shoulders, pulling me closer to kiss me back. "I think I like you too," she whispers when we come up for air.

I grin, brushing her hair from her face. "Good, because I was gonna hound you until you gave in." Seeing her so hurt before, it hurt me too, and that's when I knew I'd only feel like that if I really liked her.

She chews her lip in that way she always does when she's worried. "You're drunk. Will you still remember this tomorrow?"

"If I don't, you'll have to show me what I forgot," I say, tugging the sheets from her body and grinning down at her pink night shirt.

She blushes. "I wasn't expecting company."

"Rabbits are my favourite," I tell her, tugging at the buttons on her top. She helps by slipping her arms out and pulling it over her head. I stare at her naked breasts. "Perfect," I mutter. "You're fucking perfect."

"Are you slipping out of those jeans?" She grins as I lie back on her bed. I watch her kneel beside me and reach for the fastening. She tugs it open and pulls at the zipper, and I lift my arse so she can slide the denim down my thighs. Once she's removed them completely, she goes back to kneeling beside me. My cock is standing at its full attention, desperate to feel her hands, and when she reaches into my boxer shorts, I close my eyes and suck in a deep breath. Her hand wraps around my erection and her thumb brushes the bead of pre-cum. She spreads the wetness over the head, then slowly lowers herself until her mouth is inches away from where I'm eager to feel it.

"If you're too drunk, maybe we should wait until you're sober to do this," she whispers.

My head whips up, and when our eyes meet, she grins playfully and swipes her tongue over the head of my cock. I hiss, fisting the sheets when she sucks me into her mouth. I can't take my eyes off her. It's the most beautiful sight in the world, and when she cups my balls, I almost combust. I withstand a few more minutes before I'm flipping her onto her back and crawling up her body. There's a fire in her eyes promising me all kinds of pleasure as I pull a condom from the pocket of my jeans and rip the packet. "You sure about this?" I ask, praying to God she doesn't back out now my balls are aching for a release.

She smirks. "You're not getting cold feet, are you?"

I position myself at her entrance, then lower my head and take her nipple in my mouth. She moans, wriggling beneath me. "Never," I murmur, pressing my cock to her heat. "I'm gonna be quick. I can't help it, you're too fucking perfect. But I'll make it up to you," I push inside, and she cries out, "over and over."

The way she moans and pants between each hard thrust brings me over the edge in minutes. I know she hasn't come, and that's on me, so the second I release, I pull from her and crawl down her body, burying my mouth into her wet pussy and licking her clean. She tastes like every aphrodisiac I could ever need, and I know without a doubt, that as she comes against my tongue, I'll never look elsewhere because she's got me addicted to her, and I didn't even expect it.

We lay beside one another, panting for breath. "What about—" she begins, but I turn to the side and place my finger over her lips to silence her.

"No, don't do that. Don't cast doubt on it. Let's go with it and take our time. This is new to me. I don't pursue women like this."

"Apart from Harriett," she whispers.

I tip her chin up and kiss her gently. "We all have a past. How are we meant to find our future if we hang around waiting for something that will never be?"

"And will it . . . never be?"

I nod. "Harriett isn't interested. I like you, Nelly. Let's just try with no pressure."

She smiles, biting her lower lip. It feels good to see her smile, and I move on top of her, pulling the sheets over us and settling between her legs. "Now, I told you I'd make it up to you," I say, winking.

I wake with Nelly lying over me. My arms are wrapped around her, and the second she stirs, my cock springs to life. She shifts, looking up at me and smiling sleepily. "You're still here," she mumbles. It's another reminder how shit she's been treated in the past, the fact she expected me to be gone before she woke up.

I kiss her on the head. "Where else would I be?"

"I had a bad dream that we woke up and you were mortified," she tells me. "You ran out of here so fast."

"I was serious last night, Nells."

"It just seems to have come out the blue," she says, rolling away from me.

I frown, rolling too until I'm behind her. I pull her back into my arms and hold her against me. My cock presses against her arse. "I hope you're not running,"

I whisper against her ear, "because I will give chase, and I'm good at chasing."

"I didn't even think you liked me," she says.

"I didn't know you," I admit. "But the small amount of time I've spent with you makes me want to get to know you. Isn't that what this is?"

She nods. "I guess. But what does it mean? Is it just sex? Is it sex and dating?"

I grin. "Aren't there rules about this sort of stuff? Shouldn't we at least have a few dates before we talk labels?"

She tries to get free from my grip, and I realise she's annoyed. I hook my leg over hers, pinning her to the bed. "If you want to talk rules, we shouldn't have had sex until at least date six," she hisses.

"Six!" I gasp, cupping her breast and rolling her nipple between my finger and thumb. "I always hated rules. How about," I kiss her neck, "we go on some dates, do some more sex, and see how it goes." I run my hand down her front and part her legs using my own. I brush a finger over her sensitive, swollen bud, and she bucks. I grin at how ready she is to take me again.

"Will you have sex with other people too?"

I push a finger inside her, and she shivers. "Do you want me to?"

"Of course not. But I can't stop you. I just—"

"You can stop me, Nelly. Just say the words. Tell me what you want." I rub circles over her clit, and her breathing gets faster. "Tell me I can only fuck you."

"Is that what you want?" she whispers, pulling her pillow to her face. I tug it away from her.

"I want to see you come," I say, flicking my tongue over her erect nipple. "And for the record, Nelly, you're only gonna have sex with me, and I'm only gonna have sex with you. You wanna fuck someone else, you tell me straight and I walk away. Okay?" She nods, and I tug her nipple gently between my teeth. "I want the words."

"Yes," she hisses. "Yes, okay." Her pussy clenches around my fingers as she shudders.

"Good girl," I whisper, kissing her while she rides her orgasm.

NELLY

I lie awake in a sleepy but satisfied state while Ghost showers. Smiling to myself, I never saw it coming. And even last night, as we had sex, I had my doubts that he'd stay the night. When I woke up wrapped in his arms this morning, I hardly dared to believe it. I mean, Ghost! And after everything he said about me, I just can't believe it.

When he returns, he's still naked but wet, rubbing his hair on the towel, and I can't take my eyes from his toned body. He's gorgeous and completely perfect. "What are you doing today?" he asks.

"It's my day off. I'm meeting my parents for dinner this evening."

"Why don't you stay with me tonight at the club? I'll pick you up after dinner."

"Okay." I watch him dress.

"Will it be just your parents?" he asks casually, and I shrug. I never know with them, as they spring guests on me all the time. "Is Hugo likely to be there?" This time, he fixes me with a serious stare.

"I doubt it."

"Just remember what we agreed, Nelly. No sex with others until we figure out how we feel."

I nod. "I know."

"I don't forgive easily," he adds, looking away while he fastens his jeans. "And if we agree on no others, I expect you to stick to it."

I crawl towards him as he watches in amusement. "I hear you," I tell him, running my hands over his chest. "No one else." I kiss him, and he runs his hands through my hair, gripping it at the base and tugging slightly. Christ, I could easily do this all day with him, but his mobile buzzes and he pulls it from his pocket, breaking our kiss to check the caller id. "I gotta go. I said I'd help Harriett with her stock today. She's got a huge delivery and needs some muscle."

I smile awkwardly. It's been one night, and I can't get all bunny boiler over Harriett, but if anyone was to turn his head away from me, she would be it. He's liked her for so long. He senses my unease and kisses me again. "She's my friend, Nelly, I promise."

I force a smile and nod. "I know. It's fine. Of course, it's fine . . . I have loads to do today."

"Oh yeah?"

"Go. Honestly, go. You're needed."

He grins, kissing me one last time before heading out.

I flop back into bed and let out a sigh. It's my day off and I have no plans. Grabbing my phone, I send a text to Rylee asking if she wants to meet for lunch. I need to debrief her about the last twelve hours.

I spent the morning relaxing in bed before coming to this quaint little bar that Rylee suggested. She's already waiting as the waiter takes my coat, so I greet her with a hug, and we take a seat opposite each other. "I'm so glad you messaged me. I wanted to speak to you," she tells me.

"I wanted to speak to you too," I say.

"Me first. I know you love working at the club, but I want to offer you a different position . . . working with me at the women's centre."

I gasp. "Really?"

She nods eagerly. "Yes. I couldn't think of a better person. Mav is completely fine with me poaching you. It means no more shift work, and I can offer you full-time regular hours with full training."

"Oh my god, of course, I'd love to."

"Great! Could you start on Monday?"

I laugh. "Yes, if Mav is fine with that."

"This is so exciting," she says, grinning. "I can't wait to work with you." The waiter takes our order, and then Rylee leans closer. "So, tell me why you wanted to speak to me."

I pick at some imaginary fluff from the tablecloth. "Me and Ghost—" I begin.

"I knew it," she almost screeches.

"Easy," I say, laughing at her eagerness. "It's been one night. And we haven't labelled it or anything, but I wanted to get your advice. You're the President's ol' lady, so you know the ins and outs of the club and how things work."

She frowns. "I don't know what you're asking me, Nelly."

"How do I get it right?" I pause before adding, "Keeping him interested?"

She grabs my hand across the table. "Nelly, you said yourself, it's been one night. I don't think you need to worry about keeping his interest right now. Just be yourself."

"But after the things he said—"

"Don't think about that. It's in the past and, clearly, he doesn't feel that way deep down or he wouldn't be looking in your direction. Honestly, be yourself, Nelly, you're amazing the way you are."

"He's gorgeous," I mutter.

"And so are you."

"But I'm not in his league, Rylee. I'm not stupid."

"Are you kidding me?" she hisses. "You're beautiful."

"I've spent years watching the guys and wanting that sort of love, and now it might be in my reach, I'm scared I'll fuck it up."

"I don't see how you can. You're putting too much pressure on yourself. Just enjoy being with him and the rest will fall into place. All those guys ever need is loyalty and love."

When I get home, Ghost is on the doorstep. I can't hide my smile as I open the gate. He looks up and grins. "How long have you been waiting?" I ask.

"Not long. Where have you been?" He wraps me in his arms and kisses me.

"I met with Rylee. I thought you'd be busy all day."

Unlocking the door with his arms still around my waist, I make my way inside. He kicks the door closed and pulls me against him, burying his nose into my neck and inhaling deeply. "I missed you too much," he whispers. He glances at his watch. "I have a job in an hour."

I smirk. "So, you came by for coffee?"

He begins tugging at the button on my jeans. "If that's what you're calling it these days."

I giggle, shrugging my jacket off and dropping it to the floor. Breaking from his grip, I run up the stairs with him hot on my tail.

I arrive late to the restaurant. There are at least five other people at the table with my parents, and I wonder why the hell they invite me to this sort of thing when I'm not connected to the business anymore. They both stand and kiss me on the cheek, then introduce me to their guests. I take a seat and am just getting settled when I spot Hugo coming towards us, followed by his wife. My heart speeds up and I fidget uncomfortably while more introductions take place. Hugo sits on the chair beside me without looking at me, and his wife sits beside him.

As conversation breaks out amongst the guests, I lean closer to Mum. "Why did you invite me? I thought it was just the three of us?"

"We want to see you as much as possible whilst we're here."

"I get that, but what's the point in me coming tonight when you clearly need to entertain your business associates."

"Darling, your name is still part of the company. It's family-run."

"I left," I mutter.

"It's not like we're asking you to run meetings. We just need you to show your face now and again. Your dad and I aren't getting any younger, so maybe it's time we thought about finishing the business or handing it to you." She smiles tightly. "Karen, you remember my daughter, Nelly," she says to Hugo's wife.

I glance in her direction, wincing when her pointed features glare back at me. "Yes."

"Nelly, Karen is having her third child," Mum explains.

There's no way my face reacted the way it should, and I know without a doubt that I grimaced and gasped all at once. Karen arches her perfectly drawn brow. "Congratulations," I manage to squeeze out. "I need the bathroom." I throw my napkin down and head in the direction of the exit. Breaking out into the fresh air, I suck in a lungful, letting the cold fill my airways.

"Nelly!" It's Hugo, and I groan aloud. "I should have told you," he adds.

"Why are you out here? Can you make it any more obvious?" I snap. "Fucking pregnant, Hugo," I growl angrily.

"Just calm down."

I begin to pace. "I should have known. Why is she here?"

"She wanted to visit London for shopping."

"Course she did," I scoff.

"As far as she's concerned, we're in the past."

"She isn't fucking stupid, Hugo. We've both left the table, of course, she knows."

"I'll come over later and explain everything."

"There's nothing to explain. You have a wife. I've been so fucking stupid. Before, I was a confused teenager who believed your bullshit, but now, I'm an adult and I have to grow the hell up. We're done, Hugo. For good."

I storm back inside, stopping by the bar on the way and ordering myself a large vodka. When I take my seat, Hugo is already there, telling the guests a funny story about the last child's birth. I knock the vodka back and wave my hand at a passing waitress to request another.

I spend the dinner in silence, hardly touching my food but drinking a lot of alcohol. By the time Dad pays the bill, I'm unsteady on my feet. I go to the bathroom and pull out my phone, seeing I have three missed calls from Ghost. I dial his number just as the bathroom door opens and Hugo barges in. "Stay here. Let me drop her back at the hotel and I'll come back for you. I can't let you go home alone in that state," he snaps.

I laugh. "Now you want to play the concerned? What are you? A lover, a boyfriend? Oh god, none of those."

"Nelly, don't be angry with me. You know we're good together."

"When it suits you," I slur, pointing my phone at him. I catch a glimpse of myself in the mirror and turn side on. "Do you think I'm fat?"

He frowns. "No, you're gorgeous. Let me take you home and I'll show you," he says, wrapping his arms around my waist.

I try to shrug him off. "I can't let you in my house. I'm seeing someone."

"He doesn't have to know." He kisses my neck.

I hold my phone up so I can call Ghost, and I close one eye so I can focus on the screen. It's already lit up and I realise I've already called his number. I press it to my ear. "Ghost?"

"Where the fuck are you, Nelly?" he growls.

I shrug from Hugo's arms. "Spring Water," I tell him.

"I'm two minutes from there. You better be outside waiting when I get there. And tell your lover to fucking run." He disconnects as I swallow nervously before bringing my eyes to Hugo.

"He's not happy. I think he heard us."

"You can't have been with him that long, Nelly. Who the fuck does he think he is to order you around?"

I tuck my phone away. "He's my future," I tell him. "Goodbye, Hugo."

I step out the bathroom and straight into a slap from Karen, who is glaring at me with so much hate. I glance around for my parents, but they're nowhere in sight. "I knew you'd fuck him again," she hisses. Hugo stands beside me, looking pale and lost for words.

"I . . . I didn't know about . . ." I trail off as I point at her stomach.

"You knew about the other two though," she snaps. "You're a dirty slapper."

"He's the married one," I point out. "I'm not cheating."

"Sweetheart, remember, anger raises your blood pressure," says Hugo.

"What the fuck did I tell you, Nelly?" comes Ghost's voice.

I shiver, turning to face him. "Sorry," I mutter.

He strides towards me and grips my chin, tilting my head back and staring at the red mark I'm certain is visible on my cheek. "You're the wife?" he asks Karen, and she nods. "You hit my woman?" She nods again. "Now I don't feel so bad," he says, releasing me. He punches Hugo hard, forcing him to fall back, gripping his nose.

"Fuck," Hugo mutters as blood pours through his fingers.

"You come near her again, I'll kill you."

Ghost takes me by the hand and pulls me towards the exit. I stumble from a combination of my heels and alcohol. It annoys him, so he stops and throws me over his shoulder.

When he gets to his bike, he dumps me back on my feet. "Sorry," I mumble.

"For?" he snaps.

I frown, then shrug. "Hugo."

"Did you kiss him?"

I shake my head. "No."

He shoves the spare helmet into my hands then gets on the bike. I carefully push the helmet on and join him, wrapping my arms around his waist. I can sense his anger, it radiates off him, and as he swerves in and out of traffic, I vow not to piss him off again.

The second we get into the clubhouse, he throws me over his shoulder again so no one can speak to me. He takes the stairs two at a time, and once we're in his room, he throws me on the bed and braces himself above me. "I don't want other men near you," he pants, glaring into my eyes with a steely look. "I want you to myself. Every part of you." My heart thumps in my chest. "Hearing you and him tonight made me feel things I've never felt. I could go back there and fucking kill him with my bare hands," he snaps.

I gently stroke my hand down his cheek. "I only want you," I whisper, and he briefly closes his eyes.

"Then that's settled," he mutters. "You're mine."

CHAPTER SEVEN

GHOST

Claiming Nelly feels like the best decision I ever made. When I'm around her, my world lights up. It's been a month since I told her she was mine. A month of being buried inside of her every single night and waking every day wrapped around each other. Today, I'm surprising her by making things more official. When I roll the bike to a stop outside the tattoo shop owned by the club, Nelly removes her helmet and smiles at me. "What's this? Are you getting more ink?" I get off the bike and grab her by the hand, leading her into the shop.

"We're getting ink, baby," I tell her.

Tatts is busy drawing, but he eventually looks up and smiles. "The Riders' latest victim of love," he says, putting his pad to one side and standing. We bump fists, and then he leads us around the privacy screen.

"We're getting tattoos?" repeats Nelly, looking confused.

I turn to face her, taking both her hands. "If you're not ready, we can put this on hold, but it's gonna happen." She keeps her baby blues fixed on mine for a silent minute while I hold my breath, waiting for her to freak out. Instead, she smiles. "I'm ready. I just didn't expect it."

"I wasn't kidding when I said I'm keeping you." I grin, pulling her against me and kissing her hard.

"Get a room," mutters Tatts as he preps his equipment.

Nelly sits in the chair and begins to lower the waistband of her trousers. I still her hands. "What are you doing?"

She frowns. "How will he get to my hip if I don't lower my leggings?"

"First of all, there ain't no point having my name if no one can see it. And second of all, no man is going below this line," I run my finger across her waistband, "except for me."

She grins. "Where do you suggest I have it then?"

I take her hand in my own and turn it over, exposing her inner wrist to me. I place a gentle kiss there.

"But everyone gets theirs there," she complains.

"Not everyone. Maybe here would be best," I add, kissing her on the forehead, "that way, everyone can see who you belong to."

She laughs. "I like the wrist."

It takes Tatts just a few minutes to scroll my name on Nelly's wrist. It looks perfect, and my heart swells with pride. I've arranged to meet my parents for lunch right after this to tell them the good news. The second Nelly gets out the chair, I remove my top and take her place. I pat my chest as Tatts pulls out the piece he'd already drawn up for me. The area over my heart is the only place I don't have artwork. I've been saving it especially for this moment. Nelly watches as Tatts transfers the outline onto my skin. Her name sits proudly in large letters. "That's big," she murmurs, her fingers gently brushing the area.

"I want the world to know," I tell her.

When Tatts is finished, I stare in the mirror at Nelly's name. It's perfect. I can't wait to add our children's names around it. A whole football team's worth.

We arrive at the restaurant and find Dad already seated, his face like thunder. He hates eating out, but I didn't leave him any choice. Mum is sitting beside him, chatting to Gracie, while Scar sits with his head slightly lowered, taking in his surroundings. Dad looks up with relief when he spots us. "About time," he mutters as we shake hands. I do the same to Scar. "What's this all about?"

"All in time, Pops," I say, grinning.

"It doesn't take a genius to work it out," Mum says, taking Nelly's wrist and staring at the wrap covering the fresh artwork.

Nelly grins before looking at me to confirm. "Fine, I wanted us all here so I could tell you I'm claiming Nelly."

Scar stands and wraps me in a hug, patting me on the back. "About t-time."

"Man, it's been a month, I rushed it as it is."

"When you know, you know," says Dad, also hugging me. "Does the Pres know?"

"Of course." I told Mav last night, and he was over the moon. Nelly is already a part of the club in his eyes, so this just makes it more official.

Nelly is congratulated by the women in my life, and when we finally sit down to order, we're all smiling like lunatics. "I'm so happy for you both," says Mum.

"No pressure at all, but we'd like another grandson," adds Dad, and they smile at each other fondly. "We gotta raise the club's next generation."

"One step at a time," says Nelly.

"You don't want kids?" asks Gracie, looking surprised.

Nelly shifts uncomfortably. "Yeah, one day. But there's no rush, right?" she asks, looking at me for reassurance.

"We got a lot of kids to make, baby. Sooner we start, the better," I joke.

Nelly doesn't return my laugh. Instead, she looks down at her fingers, twisting them into knots. "You're right," says Mum, patting her hand. "It's only been a short time. Take it slowly."

"Slowly my arse," Dad grunts. "Your ma was pregnant within four months of me first landing a kiss on her and we're still going strong."

"You never did have any patience, Gears," says Mum, laughing. "He told me he wanted kids the first time we met."

"With you," Dad points out. "Only with you."

"Please, stop. I'll vomit if you don't," I tease. "Where's my annoying niece?" I hardly see Scar's eldest daughter these days.

Gracie takes Scar's hand in her own. "She's showing us that teenage years are no fun, for any of us."

"August is too sweet to cause you any problems," I say. I've always had a soft spot for her, and the fact she's nothing like her crazy mum is a miracle after she spent the first fourteen years of her life with her. She's now sixteen and spends all her time with her friends, none of whom are from the club, as the kids there are all younger.

"Sh-she's more interested in h-her friends," stutters Scar.

"Like most teenagers. You remember what Meli was like, right?"

"She told us she wants to move to Ireland to be with her mum," adds Gracie. "I'm sure it was just in anger, but it's upset us."

"Take her phone, ground her, and lock her in her room. She'll soon come around," I suggest.

"She knows Katya won't put any rules in place and she'll be free to do whatever she wants," says Mum gently. "Teenagers like to test the boundaries, but if you didn't put any in place, she'd be just as miserable. Kids like rules, they just don't know it." Katya left August with Scar and went to Ireland a few years ago. She needed time to get better, at least that's what she told Scar, though I don't think any amount of time could fix Katya. She was cruel, violent, and fucked in the head, and that was on her good days.

We eat our food and relax into easier conversation about the club and the women's centre that Rylee is running. Nelly started work there a month ago and loves every second of it. I often have to force her to come home because she gets so absorbed in the place, as do most of the ol' ladies who now help out there. It's becoming a real family affair. The brothers tend to avoid the place. Vulnerable women who turn up for help are often cautious of men, especially motherfuckers like us, so our appearances scare the hell out of them.

My mobile rings out, and as I answer, I get up from the table and step outside. "Hey, Harriett, how's things?"

"Ghost," she sniffles, "can you come over to the shop?"

I glance through the window at my family laughing and chatting. "Sure, what's wrong?"

"I got a letter from him," she says, and I know by 'him', she means her ex. "I haven't opened it yet but . . ." She trails off.

"I'm on my way," I mutter, anger coursing through me. How dare he fucking break the deal? Grim went to prison because that shithead pressed charges. The deal was, Grim would admit assaulting him, despite the fact he was protecting Harriett, if he'd leave Harriett alone. Nelly watches me as I walk back into the restaurant and chuck some cash on the table to cover the bill. "I gotta get out of here. Can one of you drop Nelly off home for me?"

"Sure," says Gracie. "Something important?" asks Dad, standing. "Club shit?"

I shake my head. "Not yet. Harriett needs me."

"Why's she c-calling on y-you?" asks Scar.

"Cos she trusts me, brother. We're friends." I place a kiss on Nelly's head. "That okay?" I ask her, and she nods. It's another reason I like her so much—she never gives me shit about other women.

NELLY

I watch Ghost leave with a heavy heart. "That happen often?" asks Gracie quietly. The others are busy chatting, but I still don't want them to overhear.

"They're just friends," I repeat his words.

We say our goodbyes and head for Gracie's car. She tells Scar she'll be home later, and he nods begrudgingly because he hates being apart from her. It's sweet.

Once we're in the car, she fixes me with a glare. "How often does he run at the drop of a hat?"

I shrug, feeling like a jealous bitch. "Maybe once a week."

"What?" she screeches. "Why?"

"I don't know. Once it was to remove a spider, another it was because her shower broke. He cares about her."

"And that doesn't bother you?"

"They're friends, and it's not my place to put a stop to it. I trust Ghost."

"I know, and he's completely trustworthy, but it's annoying she's relying on him so much. There're other brothers at the club who can help. Maybe if Mav knew she needed so much support, he'd arrange for the guys to drop by more often."

I shake my head. "I don't think that's a good idea. Ghost would have told him if he wanted help."

"We don't have to tell Ghost. We could keep it between us."

"It's not a good idea. Look, I honestly don't mind. She needs help from time to time, and Ghost is her friend. She trusts him."

Gracie smiles. "You're always thinking of others, Nelly."

When Ghost turns up at my door a few hours later, he looks stressed. I grab him a beer from the fridge and open it. "Is Harriett okay?" I ask.

"Not really. I think she's gonna stay back at the club," he says, taking the beer and drinking half the bottle.

My heart thuds in my chest. "How come?"

"To keep her safe. Her ex has been in touch. Piece of shit," he mutters angrily. "I can't leave her in that apartment alone and there's not enough room for me to stay with her, so she'll have to come and stay with me."

I knot my fingers together, and his eyes fall to my hands. "Stay with you?" I repeat.

"I mean at the club, not my room, obviously."

I force an unsure smile. "Right."

"Which is why I'm here," he adds, placing the bottle on the table and reaching for me. I let him pull me closer. "You're my ol' lady now, so you need to be at the club too."

I raise my eyebrows in surprise. "You want me to move in?"

He grins. "Of course. Ain't that what couples do?"

"Sure," I mutter, "but not so soon, Ghost."

"If I'm sure enough to claim you, I'm sure we should be together all the time. I can't have my ol' lady living away from me and the club. It ain't how we do things."

"Can I think about it?"

"What's there to think about?"

I shrug, pulling my hand from his. "It's a huge step for us both. You're not used to having a woman around all the time, and I like my own space."

"We're doing this, Nelly."

"What if you get sick of me?" I ask, worry showing on my face. "You'd feel bad kicking me out if we didn't work out because we rushed into things."

He grabs my hands again, smiling. "Is that what you're worried about? Baby, this is it for me, and yeah, we might irritate each other from time to time, nobody's perfect, but I want you in my life forever, Nelly. I want what all the other guys have, and I want that with you." He kisses me, and I smile against his lips.

"When you put it like that . . ."

"You don't have to give up this place just yet if you don't feel completely ready, but I can promise you, you won't need it."

When we get to the club, the other ol' ladies rush to greet me. Seems everyone knows about our news, and the women are especially happy for us. Ghost takes my bag to his room and leaves me to fill the women in on my decision to move in on a trial basis.

"I'm so happy for you," Rylee gushes as we sit on the couches.

"I knew you liked him," says Rosey. "I could see it in your eyes."

"Bullshit," says Meli, laughing. "You said they'd never work."

Rosey taps Meli playfully on the arm. "Hey, I'm trying to turn over a new leaf today and I'm being more positive."

"Is that what your therapist suggested?" asks Hadley.

"No, she said I'm a lost cause." They all laugh, and I sit back and enjoy the happiness surrounding me. It's been too long since I felt a sense of belonging, but I feel it here.

"And you'll be closer to the women's centre," says Rylee, "which means you can help out with emergency callers."

"She spends enough time in that place," says Ghost, returning from dumping my bag. "I need some time with my ol' lady," he adds, holding out his hand to me. I take it and let him pull me to stand. "Goodnight, ladies."

The second we get in his bedroom, he kicks the door shut and slams me against the wall. "I love having my name on your skin," he murmurs between kisses. "I love having you here with me," he adds. "And I love you." I suck in a breath. "I know you're worried I'm rushing into this, Nelly, but I love you. It's hit me hard and fast and unexpected, but I'm not wasting any more time. And I don't expect you to say it back, not until you're completely ready." He kisses me again, this time running his hands over my arse and tugging me harder against him. "Now, get fucking naked."

I giggle, reaching for the buttons on my shirt. "I'm not your personal whore just because you've claimed me," I joke. "Ask nicely." He grins, gripping the material of my shirt and giving it one hard tug. Buttons fly off and my shirt hangs open. Looking down at my exposed bra, I tell him, "You have no patience."

By the time I'm naked, he's already sheathed his cock and is watching me. "You're so fucking sexy," he growls.

"And you're insatiable."

"For you," he says, bending me over the bed and slapping my arse. He growls again and lines his erection up at my entrance. "I've been thinking about this pussy all day."

I close my eyes as he eases inside. I love his dirty mouth and the way he groans at the back of his throat every time he enters me. He takes his time, fucking me slow, like he's enjoying every second. When he's almost ready to come, he pulls out and drops to his knees behind me. Burying his face against my pussy, he grips onto my thighs to keep me exactly where he wants me while he brings me to orgasm. I come so hard, I cry out, pushing my face into the mattress as my body shakes. I'm still shuddering with aftershocks when he pushes back inside me to chase his own release.

Ghost spends the night either inside of me or wrapped around me. Not that I'm complaining. I don't remember the last time I had a man want to spend the night with me without needing to leave for someone else. And when morning comes, and he wakes me with a mug of coffee, I'm ready to explode with happiness. It's the simple things I love the most.

"I have a few collections to make this morning, but I'm free at lunch. How about I pick you up from the centre and we eat together?" he suggests.

"Yeah sure," I agree.

"I gotta take Harriett to work this morning, so I've gotta shoot." He kisses me on the forehead as he pulls on his jacket.

"Can't anyone else take her?" I ask cautiously. He stills, looking at me. "I mean, I'd like to have breakfast with you today, seeing as it's my first day at the club."

"Fuck, I didn't think of it like that," he says. "Of course, I'll go ask someone else."

I instantly feel bad. Harriett is his friend and it's just a ride to work. "Yah know what, no, it's fine. You go, I can get my own breakfast, I'm a big girl." I smile, and he looks relieved.

"Thank you. I'll make it up to you at lunch and then dinner, and I promise we'll have breakfast together tomorrow."

Gracie pats the chair beside her when I make it down to breakfast. "Good morning. How was your first night?"

I smile and blush. "Great."

"Where is the old man? Have you tied him to the bed whilst you refuel?"

I laugh. "No. He's taking Harriett to work."

"I spoke to Mav. I know you said not to bother, but it just sort of slipped out."

"Right, erm—" Before I can respond, Ghost stomps in looking pissed.

"Pres, can I have a word?" he mutters.

Mav grins. "Have several, but don't expect me to put this coffee down."

"You got Dice to take Harriett to work?"

Mav leans back in his chair and gives Ghost an easy smile. "So?"

"I said I'd take her."

"And last time I checked, I was the President. I thought you'd want breakfast with your ol' lady today."

Ghost glances my way, but I look away, praying he doesn't realise I'm sort of behind this. "Harriett trusts me, Pres."

"And she should learn to trust the other brothers too. Focus on your ol' lady and all will be well with the world. Don't you have some collections to do?"

Ghost doesn't look happy. "Yes, Pres."

"Then get on with your day. I'll be picking Harriett up from work this evening. Take Nelly out somewhere."

CHAPTER EIGHT

GHOST

I stare down at the scrap of paper with the address scribbled across it that Arthur Taylor gave me just half an hour ago. Dice gets off his bike and comes over to where I'm still sitting on mine. "Problem?"

"This place," I mutter, nodding towards the small office block. "I know this place. Nelly's dad was talking about it with his business partner."

"So," Dice shrugs, also looking at the building.

"He had a meeting here a few weeks back to sign a deal."

"Ain't nothing to do with us, brother. If Arthur's got money wrapped up here, it's between him and the customer."

I nod, getting off my bike. He's right, it's nothing to do with us. Arthur lends money to all kinds of people, good and bad, and it ain't my job to question it. Our job is to collect the weekly payments on time.

I follow Dice inside, where an older lady looks up from the front desk and gives an awkward smile. "Can I help you?"

"We're looking for," I glance at the paper, "Prescott. Tom Prescott."

"Mr. Prescott is in meetings all day."

"He's expecting us. Tell him we're here on behalf of Mr. Taylor."

A look passes over the woman's face, but I don't have time to analyse it before a door opens and a suited man rushes towards us. "It's fine, Alice, I've got this," he says sharply. "Gentleman, follow me." He leads us back into his office and slams the door. "Sorry, she's like a pit bull guarding the front desk some days. You're here for your money, yes?"

"Mr. Taylor's money," I correct.

"Of course." He fumbles about nervously with a set of keys before pulling a picture from the wall to access a hidden safe. I roll my eyes at how cliché it is. "The thing is," he continues, and I exchange a look with Dice. It's not often we have problems collecting these days. Arthur makes his rules of business very clear, and he only works with businessmen who have assets. They risk losing it all if they fuck up. "My latest clients are a little trickier than I thought they were going to be. They've gotten cold feet about our deal and—"

I hold up my hand, cutting him off. "I don't wanna hear about problems, Tom. I just need to feel the weight of that grand in my pocket as I walk out of here."

Dice begins throwing and catching the two golden dice he carries around with him. "We've already been here too long," he mutters.

Prescott pulls out an envelope, and I know it's short the second he hands it to me. I'm out of practice, so I throw it down on the desk, giving me some valuable time to think of something. "It's short," I snap.

"Only by half," says Prescott with a hopeful shrug.

"Half!" I repeat. "You want me to go back to Mr. Taylor with half? You know what he'll do to me? He'll send me right back here for half your finger to show you how much half means to him. Do you want me to take half your finger?" He shakes his head. "Me either, I'm not dressed for it. Your blood will mark this tee," I say, pulling at my white T-shirt. "So, get me the rest . . . now!"

"I tried. This couple were all set to buy into—"

"Stop fucking telling me your life story," I yell. "Get on the phone and tell someone you're gonna start losing limbs if you don't pay me."

He laughs nervously. "You're not serious about that?"

"Do you even know who you're borrowing money from? What kind of businessman are you?"

"Not a great one if he's borrowing money," cuts in Dice.

Prescott pulls out his mobile and begins making calls. I take a seat at the desk and put my feet up. This is gonna be a long afternoon. He's three calls in when a name gets my attention. "Hugo, thanks for calling me back," says Tom, like he's greeting a long-lost friend. "Any news on the deal?" I knew I'd heard the name of this place before. Prescott Properties was discussed at the party I went to with Nelly and her family. "I'm in a bit of a sticky situation, old pal," he continues. "Since the Fletchers are dragging their feet, I'm having to borrow money to keep up with the pretence." He listens while Hugo speaks, nodding occasionally even though they're not face to face. "Perfect. If you could drop it in at the office." He disconnects and announces happily, "Looks like it's your lucky day, boys."

I frown. "I think it's *your* lucky day."

A few minutes later, the office door swings open and Hugo struts in wearing a designer suit and shades. When he spots me, he lifts them onto his head. "Well, if it isn't the pretend boyfriend," he says, smirking.

Bringing my feet from the desk to the floor, I rest my arms on the desk casually and smile. "Not pretend. When are you gonna stop calling her?"

"The thing is, with Nelly, she always comes crawling back. Even when she was with the last guy, she'd hop into my bed whenever I was in town. And I was calling to let her know I'm back in London for a few days."

I stand, straightening my kutte. "I'll be sure to pass that on. I think you've got some cash for me?"

Hugo glances at Tom and the pieces fall into place. "You're a loan shark?"

"Are we taking the cash or fingers?" I snap, glaring at Tom.

"Just give him five hundred, Hugo," Tom mutters. I take the envelope from the desk, and Hugo reluctantly goes into his wallet and pulls out a bunch of notes.

"Does Nelly know what you do for a living?" he asks.

"We don't get time for much talking, but we don't have secrets," I say, smiling.

"Nelly's got plenty of secrets," he mutters, counting out five hundred and handing it over.

"Not from me."

"So, you know she can't have kids," he says to my retreating back. I clench my jaw at the new information but keep my expression neutral.

"Of course."

"It's why I didn't leave the wife in the end. I would have, but I wanted a son to carry on my business and, unfortunately, she couldn't give that to me. It's the reason her last boyfriend drank so much. Not because she couldn't conceive, but because she could and lost the baby, but then, you know all that, seeing as she doesn't keep secrets."

I leave, slamming the door. Hearing all that, whether it's true or not, makes me realise how little I really know about Nelly, and that stings.

Dice offers to drop the cash to Arthur, and I take a detour to Harriett's place. She'll be finishing up anytime soon. Grim is sitting outside on his bike, waiting to take her back to the club. "I've got it from here, brother," I tell him, slapping him on the back.

Inside, Harriett is locking the safe. "I thought Grim was here to collect me," she says.

"He was, but I needed to talk, and you're good at all that," I mutter, sitting down.

"Okay, shoot."

I watch her as she folds a few ruffled clothes on the shelf. "I just saw Nelly's ex. He said some shit about her having secrets."

Harriett laughs. "Everyone has secrets, Ghost."

"Big secrets," I continue. "Secrets that might affect our future."

She turns to me, looking worried. "Then you need to talk to her. Why are you here when you should be with her?"

"She's clearly not ready to tell me, but how do I continue like I don't know?"

Harriett sits down next to me. "Maybe you should start by telling me what the secret is."

"She can't have kids."

Harriett raises her eyebrows, knowing I want kids one day. "Then you're gonna have to tell her you spoke to her ex. You don't owe him anything, and if this is a dealbreaker for you, then you have to tell her now before she gets in even deeper."

"I want a family," I mutter, "but I want her too."

Harriett gently takes my hand and gives me a sympathetic smile. "There are other ways to have children. Until you've spoken to her, you don't know if it's true. You don't know what the issues are. And you've been together such a short time. Why don't you try talking about the subject and see if it comes up naturally?"

My mobile rings, and it's Mav. "Pres?" I answer.

"Why did you send Grim back here?" he snaps.

"Cos I needed to see Harriett."

"Brother, I'm trying to do you a favour here, and you keep screwing it up. Nelly is your ol' lady, you need to talk, then you talk to her."

"What favour?" I ask.

"I'm trying to stop you getting into shit with Nelly."

I frown. "Why would I get in shit with her?"

"Because ol' ladies don't like it when us men have other women in our lives. You know how they get when they're all talking, and Gracie told Rylee, and she got me involved, which by the way, I was pissed about. Just come home to your ol' lady, would yah!" He disconnects.

"Everything okay?" asks Harriett.

I nod, despite the anger building up in me. Why didn't she just come to me if she had a problem?

NELLY

Ghost is animalistic the second he gets home. He's crawling up the bed and over my body, kissing and nipping, growling and pulling at my clothes like he can't wait to be inside me. Once he gets me naked, he pushes his face between my legs. "Jesus," I hiss, throwing my head back. "Bad day?"

"How can you tell?" he mutters, fixing his hands under my arse and raising it like I'm his last meal. I'm soon lost in a cloud of bliss as he takes the day's frustrations out on me. "You're all I've thought about," he adds, like that's a bad thing. But before I can question him, he goes back to his main meal. He's relentless, pinning my hips to the bed and not letting up until I'm crying my way through an intense orgasm. When he's satisfied I can't take any more, he releases me and gets up from the bed. I pull the sheet over me and watch him warily. Something is off, and I've learnt over the years to let these guys tell you what they want, when they want, so I stay quiet as he disappears into the bathroom. Eventually, he returns. "If you didn't like me being there for Harriett, I'd have preferred you to tell me straight."

My heart stutters in my chest. I hate being caught out. "It wasn't like that."

"You went to my fucking president, Nelly," he suddenly yells, and I push myself to sit up. "There's nothing between me and her, I told you that."

"She calls and you go running," I explain. "But I didn't go to Mav. Gracie asked me how often that happened when you left me the other day. I was being honest because it does happen a lot, Ghost. She was trying to help."

"I get you've had problems before, but you have to trust me, Nelly. I don't want you running behind my back to the ol' ladies."

"I do trust you. I told Gracie it wasn't a thing, but I can't help feeling rejected when you leave me to rush to her aid. Would you like me leaving our date to go help some guy out?"

"No, but I'd tell you that straight. I wouldn't go to others in the hope they'd solve my problems. If this is gonna work between us, you have to talk to me."

"Maybe it won't," I snap. I begin to dress, and Ghost watches me from the doorway of the bathroom. "I don't know how to talk to you about helping your friend because it shouldn't bother me. I trust you, but it does bother me, and I can't help my feelings," I rant, pulling on my jeans and fastening them.

"Where are you going?" he asks, sighing.

"And why did you just do that?" I ask, throwing my hand out in the direction of the bed. "If you were mad with me, what the hell was that?"

"I can be mad and still crave you."

"You were disarming me," I snap. "Letting me think things were good when, actually, you were planning an attack." I head for the bedroom door, throwing it open. "That's not cool, Ghost."

I take a few steps out the room before he's behind me, pressing his front to my back and caging me against the wall in the hallway. "Where are you going?" he growls in my ear. I shiver as his gravelly voice washes over me. "We're not done talking."

"I think we are."

"I wouldn't let you go," he murmurs, nudging his nose against my ear. "I wouldn't let you leave our date to go help another guy. I'd lock you in my room and fuck sense into you."

"Caveman," I mutter.

"So, you're right, I've been out of order." He moves my hair over my shoulder and rests his chin there. "Forgive me?"

"I'm sorry I didn't speak to you about it."

"Is this our first argument?" I feel him smile as he presses his erection against my arse. "Can we do the making up part now?"

At work the following day, I'm in the office with my mind firmly on the night before and the way Ghost made me feel so loved and needed. I smile to myself just as Rylee walks in. "You look happier today," she points out.

"Ghost acknowledged he was out of order dropping everything for Harriett all the time."

"That's good. I'm glad you talked." She drops a pile of paperwork on the desk. "I've got Kelsie coming in half an hour to meet her new social worker," she adds. "I really hope she gets contact with her daughter. It's the only thing keeping her going."

I open the diary and check the room is free. "Her story breaks my heart," I admit. Kelsie, like so many other women we're trying to help, is a victim, and we're the first women to ever support her in her fight to get custody of her child.

I spend the next hour in a meeting with Hadley and a new woman to the centre who needs advice about her financial situation since she left her abusive marriage. Once that's taken care of, I hang out with some of the women we help who have dropped by to have coffee and chill. The centre is a safe space for so many, so we often get people dropping by.

Later in the afternoon, Diamond drops in with Zane, Scar's son, and I make her a coffee then join her. I've always gotten on well with her, and since Ghost and I became more official, she's made it a point to spend more time with me. "I want to arrange to meet your parents," she tells me, and I smile tightly. It isn't the first time she's raised the idea.

"I'll speak to them, but they're pretty busy."

"Nelly, stop making excuses. I got Ghost to call them. They're coming to London next week, and I want to set a date."

My insides churn. "Next week?"

"Why don't you want us to meet?"

I feel bad. "It's not that I don't want you to. I just think it's very soon to do all that kind of stuff. What if we don't work out?"

"Why wouldn't you?"

"The second I tell my parents you want to meet them, they'll assume I'm getting married and drive me insane with plans and discussions. It'll get out of hand."

"You're practically married. Ghost claimed you, that's huge."

"They won't get all that. They'll want a big wedding and a ring-" I groan. "It's all they've ever wanted for me."

"Then we'll set a date for a wedding, if it makes them happy. The sooner the ring is on the finger, the sooner you can get to work on giving me more grandbabies."

I shift uncomfortably, the way I always do when babies are brought up. "One day at a time, Diamond," I mutter.

"You do want kids?" she asks.

I feel my face redden with stress. "I haven't thought about it."

"Ghost would make an amazing dad."

"I know."

She frowns. "So, why wouldn't you want kids?"

"Not everyone wants them," I snap, and she looks taken back. "Some people just don't want children. Why is it so hard to believe?"

"Does Ghost know?"

"Why would he? We've only been together a short time, and now you're talking kids and marriage." I rub my eyes. "I have a headache," I mutter, standing. "I'll catch you later." I make an excuse to Rylee about feeling unwell, and she insists I head home early.

I've only been away from my home a few nights, but it feels like forever as I push open the front door and step inside my own space. I relax immediately. It feels good to be home, where nothing is complicated and there's no pressure. I shower, change, and pour myself a glass of wine before curling up in front of the television.

CHAPTER NINE

GHOST

"Why did you push it?" I ask Mum angrily. "You don't need to interfere. I was gonna talk to Nelly about it over dinner."

I call Nelly for the eighth time. There's still no answer, and I growl in frustration. "Try her house," Rosey suggests as she shoves a cake into her mouth. "If I needed space, that's where I'd go." I snatch my bike keys. Of course, it's where she'll be.

I stare at Nelly through her window. She's curled up asleep on her couch, looking rested and peaceful. I don't have it in me to wake her, so I carefully pick the lock on her front door and let myself in. I scoop her up in my arms, and she stirs briefly before settling against my chest. I smile to myself, she's so fucking gorgeous. Carrying her to bed, I tuck her in and place a gentle kiss on her forehead. "I'm so in love with you, Nelly Fletcher."

I get back to the club and head into the office, grabbing my laptop and sitting at the spare desk near Mav's. I feel his eyes on me, so I eventually look up. "Soz, Prez. Is it okay if I sit here?"

"Something wrong with your room?"

"I need peace. We did a collection earlier, a new guy for Arthur. Prescott Properties, you heard of that?" Mav shakes his head. "I heard Nelly's dad talking about doing business with him. I just want to check there's nothing underhanded going off. He seemed dodgy."

"Aren't her parents in property too?"

I nod. "It might be nothing, but I just got a bad feeling."

After a few minutes, I've looked over Prescott's figures, and they're not good but there's no links between his business and Nelly's family, which is a relief.

I find Harriett watching television in the main room and I sit down beside her. "Did you sort things with Nelly?" she asks.

I nod. "We talked about some stuff, not kids."

"Are you going to?"

"When she's ready. Right now isn't the time. She's freaking out."

"I'm not surprised. You've gone from zero to a hundred."

I grin. "When you know, you know."

"I guess. Where is she?"

"Mum freaked her out some more, so she's at her place tonight."

"Diamond strikes again," she mutters.

I frown. "What's that mean?"

She shakes her head. "Nothing, ignore me."

I spot August having a teenage strop with my brother, so I let her comment slide and head over to see what's happened. "You don't let me breathe," she hisses.

"If only that was an o-option," mutters Scar.

"I bet Uncle Eric would let me," she tries, and I smirk. She clearly doesn't know me at all.

"Lay it on me," I say.

"Dad says I have to be home by ten on Friday. It's a party and leaving at ten would be social suicide."

"Ten!" I repeat.

"Exactly, he's being unreasonable."

I scoff. "I'll drop you off and pick you up. Be outside by nine."

"Nine!" she screeches. "It doesn't start until seven."

"That's the deal, take it or leave it."

"I hate you all," she screams before rushing off to her room.

I fist bump my brother and sit beside him at the bar. He passes me his bottle of whiskey, and I drink straight from the bottle. "Who said teenagers were hard work?" I ask, laughing.

"She's n-not used to boundaries," mutters Scar, "K-Katya's been gone y-years, but she's still very m-much present in my daughter."

"Do you ever wonder what life would be like if you didn't have kids?" I ask.

"Q-quiet," he jokes. "Th-they drive me m-mad, but I love them b-both so m-much." He looks at me from the corner of his eye. "W-what's up?"

"Do you think I've rushed things with Nelly?"

"Yes," he says firmly.

I grin. "Don't hold back."

"Do you think y-you've rushed things?"

"Yes," I say just as firmly, and we both laugh.

"B-brother, if y-you're happy, does it m-matter?"

I shake my head. "No, she does make me happy. I like being around her, and the more time I spend with her, in her," I snigger, "the deeper I fall. I don't think she can have kids."

Scar goes silent for a long while before eventually shrugging. "There's other w-ways to have kids."

"Yeah, that's what Harriett said. But if it came to having her or having kids, I'd choose her, man. I'd choose Nelly."

Scar nods, slapping me on the back. "Good choice."

NELLY

I wake to the sun blaring in my face through my bedroom window. Stretching out, I realise I'm in my bed and sit up quickly, wondering how the hell I got here. I was definitely on the couch when I felt myself nodding off last night. "Morning, beautiful," comes Ghost's gravelly voice as he appears in the doorway holding a tray. He steps inside, laying the tray across my lap. I stare down at the pastries and coffee.

"How did you get in?" I ask.

"How do you think I got my road name?" He smirks, kicking off his boots and climbing into bed beside me. He picks a croissant and takes a bite. "We gotta talk."

That lurching feeling in my stomach chases away what little appetite I had. "Okay."

"I'm not going anywhere," he says, and I turn my head to stare at him. I was expecting him to dump me. "I know men have treated you like shit, Nelly, but I'm not one of them. I'm not going to cheat, I'm not going to leave you, and I'm not going to mess you around. I'm in this . . . one hundred and ten percent." He takes the tray from my lap and places it on the bedside table before taking my hands and staring hard into my eyes. "I really like you. I don't make a habit of having women's names tattooed on my chest. I'm in this for as long as you'll have me." He places a gentle kiss on my lips. "But I realise I'm moving way faster than you're ready for. We'll slow things down. We'll take it at your pace. No parents meeting, no planning weddings, and no kid talk."

I suck in a shaky breath. The urge to cry is overwhelming but I push it down and force a smile. "About that—"

"You don't have to tell me anything you don't want to," he cuts in.

"I want to," I reassure him. "I have polycystic ovaries, which means I may find it difficult to conceive," I explain. "And I've miscarried in the past."

"Okay," he murmurs, running his thumb over my cheek and kissing me again. "Difficult doesn't mean impossible, right? We'll think about that more when we're ready for that step. There're other ways to have children," he says, smiling. "Think of all the unloved kids in the world and what we could offer them." I nod, unable to stop the tears filling my eyes. "But let me warn you, Nelly. You run off from me again, I'll throw you over my shoulder and carry you back to the club."

"Did you put me to bed?" I ask.

"I was feeling generous. I saw you looking all tired and cute, and my anger melted away."

I bite my lower lip to hide my smile. "You think I'm cute?"

"When you're asleep and not talking."

I wrap my arms around his neck and pull him down until he's lying over me. "Spend the day with me," I say, kissing him.

"As long as I don't have to share you with the world," he replies, peeking down my nightshirt.

We spend the day in bed, only leaving to shower and use the bathroom. As the evening draws in, my stomach grumbles and Ghost laughs. "I need to feed you."

We dress and head out to a nearby burger place. Women literally stare as he passes, but he pays them no attention, holding my hand tightly in his and making sure his full attention is on me. My heart swells. It's the first time I've ever felt so loved and wanted.

Once we've ordered, he grabs my hands over the table. "When I first met you, you were so confident," he says.

"It's an act," I mutter. "I can pretend to be a hard-faced cow when, in actual fact, I'm crapping myself."

"You walked into the club and basically told Mav he was hiring you."

I smile at the memory. "He was desperate."

"And you kept the brothers in check, didn't take crap."

"I still don't," I say defensively.

"So why'd yah let Hugo treat you the way he does, or the guy before him?" I shrug, feeling exposed. "I'm not criticising," he reassures me, "I just wanna know."

"I think most girls, at some point in their life, get treated like shit by a partner. We think we're in love and we'll change them. With Rob, that's what I thought. I was going to be the one to save him from his depression and drinking problem. But I got pregnant and lost the baby, which sent him spiralling, and I couldn't save him. Hugo was a mistake after one drunken night of heartache and I needed comfort. Of course, he was there with open arms." I pause, feeling shame wash over me. "I knew he was married, but I didn't care. I was selfish. He's been in and out of my life for years, and now he's like a bad habit." Our burgers arrive and I wait for the waitress to place them down and leave before turning the questions on him. "What about you?"

"Me?" he asks, smiling.

"Don't you have anyone you regret, or a story from past relationships?"

He shakes his head, taking a big bite from his burger. "I never really had time for relationships."

"You've never had a relationship?"

"Don't sound so shocked. I'm hardly a virgin."

I grin, realising I'm his first. "Why now?"

"I'm ready now. I've spent so long looking out for Scar or running for the club, I pushed women away. Harriett was the first woman," he trails off when he sees my expression and quickly rushes to explain further, "who made me think about relationships. I realised I was ready to settle like my brothers. And then pretending to be in a relationship with you felt good. I liked it."

"Why'd yah have to look out for Scar?"

"He had trouble at school because of his stammer. Then, he met Katya and shit with her went bad and lasted for years. I hated her so much, and I could see my brother slowly disappearing until he became a shell of the man he once was."

"Wasn't there anyone you ever thought you wanted to settle down with?"

"No. I had my bed full of club girls," he says, laughing. "I was living the life of a bachelor to the fullest, and I don't regret it because now I'm ready and I've got you."

"Why me?"

"Why not you?" he asks.

I place my half-eaten burger down. "Star is gorgeous, so is Harriett. You could have anyone. Don't you see the women staring at you as you walk down the street? You could choose anyone."

"Nelly, you're the most beautiful woman I've ever met. No one comes close. I don't know why you don't see it. And I don't notice those other women because I'm too busy glaring at all the men who are looking at you."

I blush. "They do not."

"It's just you, baby. Just you."

CHAPTER TEN

GHOST

The next few weeks pass in a blur. We settle into an easy routine, spending every spare moment together. Every day, I try hard to show her how I feel about her because I desperately want her to get her confidence back.

We also managed to delay her parents' visit, so it's no surprise when Nelly gets a phone call from her mum to say they're in London. "I don't know why you get yourself in such a mess over your parents coming over," I say, throwing and catching her mobile phone as I lie lazily on the bed, watching her search the wardrobe for an outfit. "You act like they hate you."

"They don't hate me, I just feel like I disappoint them," she explains, holding up a denim dress. I shake my head, and she shoves it back into the wardrobe and continues her search.

"They don't know what happened between you and Hugo, so what else did you do to make them disappointed?" I ask, smirking.

"I wasn't an easy teen."

"Was anyone? Parents don't hold grudges, Nelly. Besides, they're really nice to you. I think you're imagining it all."

She sighs heavily, then flops down beside me. "I had a twin," she mutters, and my eyes widen in shock. "She died when I was eight. Lucy. She was perfect in every single way. She was beautiful, clever, funny . . . the whole package. I never quite compared."

"Jesus, Nells, why didn't you tell me this before?"

She shrugs. "It never came up."

"You make that kind of shit come up. That's something you share, baby." I gently place a kiss on her forehead.

"Sorry. I keep a lot of things from my past close. It's not that I don't trust you, but I hate putting a downer on things, and talking about Lucy kind of brings a cloud with it."

"But it shouldn't. You should talk about her all the time and celebrate the life she should have had."

"That's just it. It should have been her here, not me, and now I feel like I shouldn't quite live my life too much because I don't deserve it." She sucks in a shaky breath and then stands again. "Gosh, that got dark quickly. You see, the cloud always comes. Now, what should I wear?"

I frown as she goes back to pulling out different clothes. "Nelly, you can't just—"

She turns, giving me a watery smile. "Another time, Ghost. Please."

I nod and decide to let it go. She'll talk when she's ready, though whatever happened to Lucy is clearly still weighing heavily on her shoulders.

Charlotte and Adam are already seated at the restaurant when we arrive. It's early evening, and after spending the day wrapped around each other between Nelly's outfit try-ons, we're both exhausted. We do the usual greeting, and Adam shakes my hand while eyeing my kutte with interest. I'd always removed it before and only Hugo had seen me in it. It's surprising he didn't break his neck to tell them their daughter was dating a biker. "It's great to see you both," he says as we sit down.

"After you cancelled the last visit, we thought you'd broken up," says Charlotte.

"That'll never happen," I say, throwing my arm around Nelly's shoulders.

"Interesting jacket," says Adam. "Is it new?"

"About that," Nelly begins, fidgeting beside me. She shrugs my arm away. "Eric helps with loads of great charities, and he plays a huge part in helping women flee from domestic violence." I frown but remain quiet as she blabbers on nervously. "He supports them after fleeing, and even keeps check on them to make sure they're coping and safe."

"Admirable," says Adam stiffly. "What's that got to do with the jacket."

"Kutte," I correct.

Nelly jumps in again. "The club he works for, they all help too. They have fundraisers and help out in the community." Her reluctance to be honest cuts me deep. Her shame and embarrassment is written all over her face.

"I'm a biker," I say firmly. Nelly stiffens, her mouth opening and closing like a goldfish. "My club is called The Perished Riders MC."

"A biker?" repeats Charlotte. "I thought you said he was working in finance?"

"I occasionally run my eyes over the books for the club," I admit.

"So, you don't work in a bank?" Adam asks. I shake my head. "Why did you lie?" he asks, turning to look at Nelly.

"I didn't lie. He . . . erm, well, he once worked in a ba—"

"Because she didn't think you'd approve," I cut in, tired of her bullshit lies. "It's only been a few months, and she needed time to build up courage to reveal the real me."

"And that's a biker," says Charlotte again, seemingly hung up on that fact.

"Who does charity work?" Adam adds, and I nod. "A couple of months?" he then repeats, frowning. "You said you'd been together for years."

"He's confused," says Nelly. "We were on and off."

"Jesus, Nelly," I snap, and she knots her fingers together nervously. "Stop with the lies. Are you ashamed of me?"

She shakes her head. "No . . . I just—"

"Then tell them the truth. Your parents aren't going to hate you because you love a biker. I'm not a bad person."

"Why would you ever think we'd hate you?" asks Charlotte, resting her hands on Nelly's. "We only ever want you to be happy."

I stand, pulling out my wallet and dropping some cash on the table. "Maybe spend this dinner as a family, catch up on reality," I mutter. "I'll join you next time, if Nelly isn't too embarrassed by me." I walk out before anyone can object.

I ride straight back to the club and open a bottle of whiskey. "That was a sh-short dinner," says Scar.

"Where's Nelly?" adds Dice.

"With her parents, explaining why she fucking wraps herself in lies."

"Okayyy," says Dice, dragging the word out. "You wanna talk?"

"To you?" I ask, laughing.

"Nah, I was gonna call Star over," he says, grinning.

"When it's just me and her, nothing matters," I admit, taking a gulp from the bottle. "But throw normal shit in, like her parents, and she gets all jumpy. I don't get it."

"Chicks are complicated, brother," says Dice.

"H-how do you know?" asks Scar, laughing.

"I've had my fair share of woman drama. They're all fucking crazy, which is why I avoid them like the plague."

"I don't wanna avoid her. I want all the shit that comes with settling down," I say, taking another drink. "I want kids and the normal stuff that you get with marriage. But she gets weird about it all, and I don't know what's going on in her head sometimes."

"Maybe just ask her?" suggests Harriett as she approaches. I take Ivy from her, and she snuggles into my chest. "Why aren't you at dinner with her parents?"

Scar and Dice leave, and Harriett takes a seat beside me. "Long story short, she lied to them about me, but tonight, I set the record straight."

"You told them you were a biker?"

"Why should I lie? I'm not ashamed."

"But you think Nelly is?" she asks.

"Isn't that obvious? She sat there in a panic, trying to sell me in a good light. Told them what a good Samaritan I was."

Harriett laughs. "So, you're upset she told them nice things about you? Would you have been happier if she told them some bad stuff too?"

I shrug. "Maybe." I sigh, placing a kiss on Ivy's head. "If we're serious, she needs to be honest with them. I can't spend my life pretending to be a banker."

"I get that, but shouldn't you have talked about it with Nelly first? Let her explain things to them herself, in her own time?"

I shake my head. "No. It needed to be done, and if she's got a problem with that, maybe it isn't going to work for us."

Harriett looks past me and winces. "Nelly," she greets.

I turn to face my ol' lady. She's pissed, I can tell by the way her eyes are boring into me. "I got a cab," she spits out. "Thanks for waiting."

"I was giving you time to explain yourself," I snap, and Ivy flinches. I soothe her with another kiss, then pass her back to Harriett.

"Thanks for the heads-up on that too," she snaps, heading for the stairs. I groan and follow after her. "A warning would have been nice if you were going to out me like that."

"You're fucking ashamed of me," I hiss. "You were tripping over your lies to paint me in a better light. Aren't I good enough?"

"That's not what I was doing." She shoves the bedroom door open, and I follow her inside, slamming it closed. "You know the stigma that comes with bikers, I didn't want them jumping to conclusions."

"I don't care what they think, Nelly. We know the truth and that's all that matters."

"I care!" She pulls off her jacket, throwing it on the chair. "And then I come home to find you soothing Harriett's kid while you pour your heart out to her?" I roll my eyes and regret it instantly when she spots me. "Oh, I'm sorry," she grits out, her voice dripping with sarcasm. "Shouldn't I let it bother me that you're talking about our relationship with another woman?"

"She's a friend."

"Bullshit!" she screams, taking me by surprise. "You were in love with her, so don't tell me she's just a friend. You wanted a whole lot more with her before me."

"*Before* you!" I shout. "Not anymore."

She removes her dress and throws it with her jacket. I'm momentarily distracted by the black lace, which only angers her more. "Don't even think about touching me," she growls.

I hold my hands up and scoff like the idea is absurd. "I wouldn't dream of it when you're acting like Satan."

"Maybe you're right, Ghost," she says, taking a calming breath. "Maybe it's not going to work."

I know I was the one to originally say it out loud, but hearing it fall from her mouth hurts. "Don't start acting crazy," I mutter, watching her warily as she pulls on some joggers.

"You just said the exact same thing."

"I wasn't thinking straight."

"Or you were wanting Harriett to jump in and tell you that maybe you're right, maybe me and you will never work, so then you've got a glimmer of hope with her?"

"Nelly, for the love of God, I love you. I love you. I don't know how many times I should say it a day before you fucking believe me. I LOVE YOU!"

"But you confide in her," she mutters bitterly.

I growl angrily. "I can't keep doing this with you. There is nothing between Harriett and me. She's my friend."

"Like Hugo's my friend?" she asks, arching a brow. I ball my fists, trying hard to keep my anger at bay. "Because you check my phone daily, making sure I haven't been in contact with him."

"That's different," I mutter.

"I don't see how. He was my friend, and I stopped all contact so I didn't upset you."

"You were fucking him—you were never friends."

"You don't know what we talked about, how we were when we were together, just me and him."

"Stop," I warn.

She narrows her eyes, and I know I've only pushed her to bait me further. "We'd lay in bed talking, between fuc—"

She doesn't get to finish her sentence because I push her against the wall and kiss her. I slam my hands either side of her head to release some of the tension. "You wanna talk about fucking other people?" I whisper against her mouth. "You want to put images in my head that will drive me fucking insane with jealousy?" I kiss her harder. "Do it. Tell me about all the times he fucking used you before going back to his wife. And I can tell you all the club girls who have sat on my cock," I hiss, pressing my forehead against hers.

"And we'll both get angry and shout. I'll probably smash something to stop me killing him, we'll fuck in temper, and I'll leave my mark on you to show the world you're mine." I move my lips to the delicate skin of her neck and nip at her. "You'll cry, I'll spend the night in the bar getting drunk, and tomorrow, we'll have a day of make-up sex. But those images we put in one another's heads will stay, the words we spat in anger will play on repeat, and we'll both be a little more bitter towards one another. We'll smile while dying inside, until eventually, we can't hide it with sex and kisses. I don't want a toxic relationship with you, Nelly. I watched Scar go through it for years. And I know all the others before me taught you that jealousy was love, they showed you that fighting was the only way to feel something, but it's not. So, we're not doing this your way because my way is better."

I take her face in my hands and use my thumbs to smooth a stray tear across her cheek. "I love you. But right now, we're both angry and upset. So, I'm gonna give you space, and tomorrow, when we're calm, we'll talk about this. Okay?" I kiss her lightly on the lips, and she nods. "I love you so hard."

"Like the most ever?" she whispers, and my heart lifts a little. It's the first time she's acknowledged me saying it.

"Like the most ever," I confirm.

"I love you too." I'm so shocked, I stutter. If things weren't so charged right now, I'd wipe out what I just said and fuck her senseless.

"Call me if you need anything." I press a final kiss to her lips and head out.

NELLY

I cry. I sit on the bed and cry the second Ghost steps out of the room. I don't want space, I just want him, and I don't know how to make him see that I'm so goddamn terrified of him leaving me that I fight myself on a daily basis not to be the overbearing, crazy girlfriend my brain begs me to be.

Rosey bursts in minutes later. "Ghost sent me," she says, wrapping her arms around me, and I smile to myself. He still sent someone to be with me even though he's mad. "Are you okay?"

I push to sit up and then tell her everything, from my lies snowballing to his time spent with Harriett and how insecure it makes me feel. When I gulp a lungful of air, she smiles and rubs my hand. "I see why Ghost didn't want me to come." I frown, and she adds, "I was the only one available. Do you want me to kill him?" It's what she does to earn a living, so I can't blame her for offering.

I laugh, shaking my head. "No, I really like him."

"Damn it, Cupid is always getting in my way." Her smile fades and her expression turns serious. "Ghost really likes you, Nelly. I don't see him ever hurting you or running away with Harriett, or any other woman for that matter. He's a pain in my arse, but he's a good guy, and you won't often hear me saying that about a man."

"I hurt him today," I admit. "I didn't mean to. I was trying to tell my parents all the amazing things he does, and he assumed I was ashamed."

"Were you?"

"No," I screech. "Not even a little. I just wanted them to love him as much as I do."

"You really need to talk to him, Nelly. Communication is key, apparently, if you want a relationship to work."

I grin. "How do you know that?"

"Hadley was lecturing Maverick earlier today when he upset Rylee. It must be a full moon out there this week—everyone's getting their knickers in a twist over relationships."

I wake with a start, sitting up and automatically looking beside me to find the bed still empty on Ghost's side. Checking the alarm clock, I see it's three in the morning. I grab one of Ghost's shirts and head downstairs to find him. Usually if the men are in the doghouse, they take a couch in the main room rather than make up a new bed in the spare rooms. It's pure laziness, but they wouldn't dare ask any of the other ol' ladies to help them out.

I find him sleeping soundly on the couch with his kutte over him. A few couches down, Maverick is sleeping, and I smile to myself. Rylee must have kicked him from her bed for the night. I gently kneel on the floor beside Ghost and run my hand over his face. His eyes shoot open, and when they land on me, he visibly relaxes. "Morning," I whisper. "I miss you."

He glances at his watch, then rubs his eyes. "You should be sleeping," he mutters, his voice hoarse from just waking up.

I nod. "I know, but I woke, and you weren't there."

"We're fighting," he reminds me, carefully tucking some stray hair behind my ear. I turn my cheek into his touch and briefly close my eyes.

"I don't want to fight anymore."

"That's not how it works," he whispers, a small smile playing on his lips.

I run my hand over his cheek and lean closer until our lips are inches apart. "I love you." I kiss him, slowly at first to test the waters, and when he doesn't push me away, I take it deeper, thrusting my tongue into his mouth and gripping his shirt in my fists. It feels like forever since I felt him inside me, and I'm not used to not having him in the bed. My hands begin to wander down his body while our lips make up for lost time.

Using one hand, I unclip his leather belt. "Baby, you're distracting me," he murmurs against my lips.

"I know."

"Sex won't make our problems go away," he adds.

I nod, unfastening his button and zipper. "I know."

"And my Pres is right over there."

I grin, pushing my hand inside his jeans and wrapping it around his hard erection. "I know."

I rub his shaft, and he closes his eyes, arching his back off the couch and hissing in pleasure. I smile smugly at his reaction. He needs me too. Make-up sex is the best kind, and I tug his jeans lower to allow his erection to spring free. I use both hands to hold it and lick him just how he likes it. He breathes heavily, lifting his head slightly to watch as I envelop his cock in my mouth. Occasionally, he looks back to where Mav is still sleeping like a baby, and when he's satisfied his Pres isn't watching, he brings his hooded eyes back to me to watch the show.

I link my fingers to give me a tighter grip on him, and then I run my tongue over his balls. He growls, fisting my hair and thrusting up into my grip. When I feel his cock swell, I push him back into my mouth and take him as far as I can, opening up my throat and allowing him to fuck my mouth. He squeezes his eyes closed and pants, thrusting hard one last time before his warm cum floods my mouth. I swallow every last drop.

CHAPTER ELEVEN

GHOST

"Fuck, that was hot," I whisper, checking Mav's still asleep. "And I want to repay the favour, but I know you can't be quiet."

Nelly gives me a mischievous grin and stands. The shirt of mine she's wearing falls open and she's naked underneath. My cock gets hard again despite its orgasm just seconds ago. "You're trying to kill me," I mutter, grabbing her thigh and tugging her towards me. When she's close, I tap her leg, and she lifts it. I guide it over my shoulder, and she hovers over my face. The sight of her wet pussy makes me grab a handful of her arse and bury my face against it. She gasps, holding the back of the couch for balance.

"Jesus," growls Mav, jumping from his couch while covering his face. I pull Nelly's shirt tighter around her to hide her body even though he isn't looking. "Now I gotta go beg Rylee to let me in the bed before I bust a nut in my pants." He storms off towards the stairs, and Nelly blushes, giggling.

I open the shirt wide and cup her breasts, tugging her nipples gently while I taste her juices on my tongue. She gets into rhythm, rubbing herself against my mouth and beard, occasionally moaning in pleasure. She stiffens, trembling as her orgasm ripples through her. I wait for her to relax before guiding her down my body so she can lie over me. She's exhausted, and I suspect she spent a few hours crying before she slept. Her eyes are still swollen.

I run my hand up and down her back, trying to ignore the way my cock strains to get inside her. She wriggles lower until I'm at her opening. "Do you have a condom?" she whispers. I shake my head even as I'm pushing up to meet her. "Maybe we should go upstairs," she adds. But I'm already inside, letting her tight, warm pussy grip my cock like a vice, and I know there's no way I'm moving off this couch until I've fucked her.

"You're my ol' lady still, right?" I ask. It's a shitty move because I know she's insecure and wants me to confirm we're okay. She nods, and I smile. "Then fuck me like it." She sits up, placing her hands against my chest, and begins rocking back and forth. She slides up and down my shaft, taking every bit of pleasure she can, and I watch her come apart again. It's like an aphrodisiac, and once she's back to being exhausted, I wrap my hands around her lower back and thrust up into her. She's got nothing left to give as she grips my shoulders, with her head buried against my chest, and I fuck her senseless. Not stopping until I come, I hold my cock deep inside her and fill her with my seed, cos if she's mine, I'm keeping her, and she'll damn well have my kids.

NELLY

I wake in bed wrapped in Ghost's arms. He's holding me so tight, we're practically stuck together. I ease from him, and he reluctantly releases me. The stickiness between my legs is a sign that we really didn't use protection in the early hours and it wasn't a dream. A part of me is mortified I could be so stupid when we're clearly having issues, but another part of me is hopeful because it means he wants to be with me forever. He wants a family with me, and even though it may be a struggle for me to conceive, it's not impossible.

"I need to shower and get to work," I say, sitting up. He throws his leg over me, and I lie back down. Pinning me beneath him, he takes my nipple in his mouth. "Ghost, I have to go." He nudges my legs apart and continues to nip and kiss across my chest. "Are you even awake?" I ask, laughing.

He thrusts into me, and I cry out in surprise. "Fully," he murmurs.

After we're both panting and sweaty, he drops down beside me. "We should talk."

"After work," I tell him, climbing from the bed and heading for the shower.

He follows me. "Now."

"Ghost, I have work in an hour."

He steps into the shower behind me, and I groan. "No more," I protest as he lathers soap in his hands and begins to wash me. He smiles innocently, but it's what he always does right before he ravishes me in the shower.

By the time I get to work, twenty minutes late, I'm tired but relaxed. Rylee looks just as relaxed when I pop my head into her office. "Good morning," I greet.

She smirks. "I hear you were taking your relationship into your own hands last night," she says.

"Mav didn't come back downstairs, so I guess he worked his magic on you?"

She blushes, laughing, "Did you sort things?"

"Not really. He wants to talk tonight over dinner."

"Dinner?" she repeats. "A biker who takes you to dinner? He's a different breed."

"Tell me about it."

It's a busy day, with several meetings running back-to-back for Rylee. I sometimes wonder if she's taken on too much, but at least after some more training, I'll be able to support her more and take on a bigger role. All plans for me that don't include babies right now. I subconsciously run my hand over my stomach. I want this career opportunity so badly, and I know Rylee would support me, maybe keeping my job open, but I've waited so long to find something where I can make a change and this is it. My thoughts are interrupted when Ghost pops his head around the door. "Penny for 'em," he says, grinning.

I gasp. "Is it that time already?"

"I asked Rylee if I could get you early. I thought we could go for a walk first."

I check my watch. "Rylee's been flat out all day, Ghost. I can't leave early. She's in her final meeting."

"She said it was fine."

I take a patient breath. "She's too nice to say no. Please don't do things like that without asking me first," I mutter.

He sighs heavily before letting the door close and heading back towards his bike. He means well, but I don't need him to control my life like that. And maybe I'm feeling a little snippy now the reality of what we did is setting in.

It's right on five o' clock when both Rylee and I step from the centre and lock up. She gives me a quick hug and whispers, "Good luck," before heading towards Mav's bike. Ghost hands me the spare helmet without looking at me, and I get on his bike. He can tantrum all he likes, but this is my job and I don't need him meddling.

The restaurant is quiet. It's still early, but I'm hungry, so the second we're seated, I pick up the menu to scan for something wholesome. After a minute or two of silence, Ghost places his menu down, and I feel his eyes burning into me. "I feel like we're taking two steps forward and fifty back some days."

I reluctantly place my menu down too. "You're too full on."

"Fuck," he mutters, "get straight to the point, why don't yah."

"You seem to have this whole thing worked out in your head, Ghost, and it's like you're forgetting to tell me about it. It's your relationship and I'm just here for the ride."

"I can't help knowing what I want."

"What about me? What about what I want?"

"I wouldn't know because you don't tell me," he hisses.

The waiter places a jug of water on the table for me and a beer for Ghost. I thank him because Ghost is too busy glaring at me to look up. "I don't want to scare you off with demands about the future. It's normal to hold back in a new relationship. It's only been a few months and we're already having unprotected sex. We didn't even discuss it."

"Maybe I got carried away," he admits. "And the chances are, you won't even get pregnant."

"Now we're taking chances? What if I do get pregnant?"

He grins. "I'd be fucking over the moon."

"You don't know me well enough to want kids with me."

"So, tell me," he snaps. "Tell me all of it. Lucy, your parents, Hugo, Rob. Tell me so I know it all and you can stop using it as an excuse to push me away."

I twist my fingers together. "That's not what I'm doing," I mumble.

"Really? Because one minute, it feels like we're full on and you're in this one hundred percent, and the next, you're pulling back and telling me I'm too full on."

"Whenever I . . . settle . . . when my guard fully comes down, that's when I get hurt. It's when Hugo told me he was staying with his wife. It's when Rob first started hurling drunken insults at me. I'm scared that if I give you everything, you'll leave me." It feels good to admit it out loud, like a weight's been lifted.

"I'm nothing like those men in your past, Nelly. I don't play games or hit out with nasty words. I'm not married or hiding anything from you. I just want you. I want us to make a real go of this because I'm ready . . . I'm ready for us to settle down."

"You say all the right things and you reassure me, but eventually, I'll drive you mad with my accusations and my insecurities."

"There you go again, trying to convince me it's best if I leave you. I'm not giving up, Nelly, so stop trying to push me away."

The waiter returns, and I order salmon. Ghost orders steak and then grabs my hands over the table. "I love you. You might think it's too soon, but I do."

"I love you too," I repeat, and he smiles. "I wasn't ashamed of you with my parents. I was worried they'd judge you without knowing the facts. I didn't mean for it to sound like it came across."

"People will always judge me, Nelly. I'm used to it. I don't care what anyone thinks. You gotta get used to that if you're gonna be with me."

"But it's so unfair when you're as amazing as you are. I've dated men who are seen as upstanding citizens and they turned out to be less than half the man you are. They don't get judged badly."

"I know I'm a good person, most of the time." He winks. "I don't need to convince anyone."

"My parents are important to me. I want them to see you like I do."

"They'll only see that by spending time with me. What did they say after I left?"

"That I was being ridiculous, and they just want me to be happy."

He smirks. "I told you that."

"Then they invited us to a charity ball next weekend." I grin, knowing he'd hate something so fancy. "It's a tux kind of night."

He groans. "I guess it comes with dating you."

"We really don't have to go," I say, laughing, "but it's sweet you'd consider it."

"Tell me about Lucy," he mutters.

I take a deep breath. I think about her all the time but talking about her is hard seeing as my parents never did. Once she was gone, it was like she didn't exist. "We weren't identical," I start, and he relaxes against the chair, his expression one of relief that I didn't shut his request down. "She was a nightmare," I add, fondly. "Always in trouble, always covered in dirt from digging in the garden. She drove Mum mad. Dad said she was the son he never had." I laugh to myself at the memory.

"She was a bad influence, always getting me to do daring shit we weren't allowed to do, like riding our bikes to the shops about a mile away. We did it a couple of times before Mum caught us, and she went mad, really mad. She banned us from having our bikes out of the shed unless she or Dad was around to supervise. Lucy was pissed, told Mum she hated her. Anyway, a few days later, Mum was ill. She was asleep on the couch, and Lucy convinced me it would be a good idea to cheer her up by going to the shops and getting her some flowers and a few of her favourite snacks. I knew it was wrong, but Mum was so ill, and I wanted to cheer her up. So, I helped Lucy get our bikes from the shed, and we rode all the way to the shops like we had a dozen times. We dumped our bikes outside the shop, and I ran ahead."

I pause, remembering the sound I've tried so hard to forget. "The bang as the car rammed into her was the worst sound I've ever heard. I can't even find anything to compare it to, and I knew, I just knew that car had hit her even though I never saw it. And then everyone began screaming and running around, and I froze. I turned and just stared at the spot outside where our bikes had been, where Lucy had been, and then I saw her hand sticking out from under the car."

"Jesus, Nelly. I'm so sorry," Ghost whispers, taking my hands again.

"A neighbour ran to get Mum. She was there before the ambulance, but it made no difference. Lucy was dead on impact. The driver ran the second the car hit her, and we never got justice."

"That's gotta be hard," he mutters.

"What's harder is they never talk about her. They didn't yell at me for going to the shops, they didn't even ask why we went. They just stopped talking. And after the funeral, everything went back to normal . . . just without Lucy."

"You didn't talk about any of it?"

I shake my head. "No, and we haven't since. If I mentioned Lucy, the room would go quiet, and everyone would look sad again, so I just stopped because I didn't want to remind them of what I did."

"Baby, you didn't do anything. You were just a kid."

"But I was the good one. I knew we shouldn't have gone to the shops. It's exactly what my parents were thinking. I went along with it, and if I'd have just said no, she'd still be here now."

"You don't know that, Nelly. She might have gone alone anyway. She might have died another day. You can't live thinking what might have been. You were just kids doing what kids do, and the only person to blame is the fucker who drove that car and ran off like a coward. Jesus," he hisses, "you've been carrying this guilt around for all these years. Your parents should have helped you through it."

"They were getting through it themselves, barely."

"It was their job as your parents to make sure you were okay, and they didn't. And you're still here trying to please them, trying to make up for something that was never your fault."

CHAPTER TWELVE

GHOST

I'm mad as hell at Nelly's parents for letting her grow up with this much guilt. They have no idea how messed up she is because of it. Our food arrives and we eat in silence, both processing her story. I'm halfway through my steak when I place my cutlery down. "What did you do at your parents' firm?"

"Messed up is what I did," she mutters.

"You fell for the wrong guy," I correct.

"He was married," she reminds me. "I shouldn't have gone there."

"He shouldn't have gone there. Fuck, Nelly, why do you take the blame for everything? He did wrong, he was the one who made a commitment to someone else. Did you chase him?" She shakes her head. "So, he pursued you?" She nods. "Then he was in the wrong first. And then his wife finds out and what?"

"She threatened to tell everyone in the office. Including my parents."

"And you couldn't bear to let them down again," I say, "even though you never let them down in the first place."

She nods sadly. "They're so fixated on me settling down, having children. How could I tell them I was sleeping with their business partner? A married man? I made an agreement with his wife. I'd move away, leave the firm, and get on with my life, leaving Hugo alone. I told my parents I'd met someone and wanted to move to London to be near him. They were over the moon, so I settled with the first guy I found. Rob."

"And that didn't go well either?"

She shakes her head again. "Nope. He was great when he was sober but a real shit when he was drunk. I got pregnant quick but lost the baby. He was devastated and used it as an excuse to drink even more. He became unbearable, so I left him too. I didn't have the heart to tell my parents, so I just avoided the conversation. Until I couldn't, and that's when I got you involved."

"And here we are," I say, smiling.

"Here we are."

"We needed this talk," I tell her, picking up my cutlery, "so we can move forward."

"Harriett makes me feel insecure," she blurts out, and I eye her for a few seconds. "I know you say you don't like her like that, but how can you just turn it off?"

"I didn't," I say, and she frowns. "But I started noticing you more and her less and it just happened. It just turned itself off."

"She can give you things I probably can't, like kids."

"I don't want her. Kids or not, I want you, Nelly. Just you."

"You look good together, better than we do."

I grin. "Now, you're just talking crap. How can anyone look better on my arm than you? You're my queen, and no one compares." A small smile plays on her lips. "I don't see anyone else but you, baby."

Things improve over the coming weeks. I make more of an effort to be considerate towards Nelly's feelings of Harriett and pull her into our conversations often. When Mav tells me Harriett is safe to return home, it's a bittersweet moment. I'm relieved that I don't have to worry about upsetting Nelly, but also worry that Harriett's ex will reappear again. Harriett is over the moon to be going home. The club never really suited her, and she loves her apartment above the boutique. Mav installed a panic button in the apartment that connects to the club, so if she presses it, we can talk to her and hear everything that goes on. It means we can head over to her rescue or call the cops, and it makes Harriett, and me, feel a little better.

It's the middle of the night when Nelly climbs over me, rubbing herself against my erection. I still her, groaning. "Baby, I'm out of condoms," I whisper.

"Then go ask someone," she replies, rubbing herself faster.

I close my eyes. "I can't go waking the guys up at four in the morning. Yah know, maybe it's time we talked about forgetting the condoms," I try. We haven't discussed it since our last slip up.

My cock brushes her entrance, and instead of moving away, she grinds over me, letting me slip inside her. I guess she doesn't need a discussion after all as she eagerly fucks me.

NELLY

"And just like that, we're trying for a baby," I tell Rylee who stares at me wide eyed. "I know it's soon, but he's so keen, and I really love him."

"Hey, I'm not judging. You do you, but are you sure it's what you want?"

I raised the topic with Ghost this morning. I told him my concerns for my career, and he happily agreed to help out with child duties whenever I decide to return to work. "Yeah, I want a family with Ghost. He'll be a great dad."

"I'm pleased for you. You both seem to be crazy in love lately. It's good to see Ghost so happy."

"He's even agreed to come to a black-tie event next weekend. My parents are retiring to a villa in France and they're having a retirement party." I was shocked when Mum called to tell me they were selling their share of the business to Hugo. I thought they'd be part of it until they were too old to walk and I'd have to force them to sell, but they seem keen, and luckily, Hugo told them about a new building project in France. They've secured a villa, and when the project is complete, they'll be moving out there.

"That sounds like heaven. I'd love to get a villa somewhere fancy. Ghost looks good in a suit," says Rylee.

"I'm excited."

"Make sure you get some photos. Men like Ghost don't dress up nearly enough, and we need evidence."

"Who's bought the family business?" asks Ghost as we dress for their retirement party.

"Hugo," I say, running my fingers through my hair to loosen the curls.

"Doesn't it bother you? I mean, you could have taken over."

I shake my head. "Not at all. I never wanted to work in property. I'm terrible at sales and I certainly don't want the responsibility of taking over their empire.

He's their partner, it makes sense for him to take over."

He kisses me on the head. "I'm glad. I'd have hated you working alongside Hugo."

I grin. "It never would have worked."

I take his tie from his fumbling fingers and begin knotting it. "So, they've already bought the villa in France?"

"Why are you so keen on the details?"

He shrugs. "Just wondering. Have they been to see it?"

"I should imagine so. They're pretty careful with money. I can't see them investing if they didn't know every single detail." I smile. "Are you worried about my parents?"

"You just hear stories about conmen doing that sort of thing."

I kiss him. "You're so sweet."

We take a car to the venue, a stately home my parents have rented for the evening. It's so beautiful, and as I hook my arm into Ghost's, I realise that I'm happy. For once, I'm settled and happy.

We find my parents in the great hall chatting with friends. The second Mum sees me, she embraces me. "You look amazing," she says, taking my hand and spinning me like she used to when I was a child. The short black dress isn't something I'd ever wear if I was out alone, but with Ghost, I know I'm not going to attract the wrong kind of attention, and the risk paid off because Ghost was more than appreciative when I showed it to him.

Dad joins us, greeting Ghost the exact same as he always does, which is a relief. I'm pleased they don't see him any different since they learnt the truth about him being a biker. "What's the villa like?" asks Ghost when Dad begins telling us how excited he is to retire.

"It's still being built," Mum explains.

"You haven't been out to see it?" I ask, frowning. "Not even the plot of land or the builders?"

"We've seen the plans. It's beautiful. And there's plenty of room for you and Eric to come and stay. And, of course, we'll keep a spare room free for grandchildren," she jokes.

I roll my eyes and smile. "When do you plan to move out there?"

"We don't have an exact date," Dad replies, "but roughly by Christmas."

Ghost's phone buzzes, and he glances at the screen before pushing it into his pocket. "Have you laid down your money yet?" he asks, and Dad looks uncomfortable. "Sorry, I don't mean to pry, I'm just interested in how this sort of thing works."

"We've put a sizable deposit down to reserve the villa, yes. They're very popular, and we didn't want to miss out."

Ghost's phone buzzes for a second time and he sighs heavily before checking it. "Take it," I say, smiling. "It's fine."

"It can wait," he insists.

A man approaches alongside Hugo. I slip my hand into Ghost's and lower my eyes. I don't want to see Hugo let alone speak with him. "Ah, here's the main man now," says Dad, shaking hands with the suited man. "Tom, meet my daughter, Nelly, and her partner, Eric." We both shake hands with Tom, and he leans in, kissing my cheek.

"Great to meet you. I've heard a lot about you, Nelly."

He gives me creepy vibes, and I smile tightly, clinging to Ghost's hand. "Eric was just asking about the villa," Dad explains, and Tom shifts uncomfortably. "You might be able to make another sale, since he seems keen," he adds jokingly.

A look passes between Tom and Ghost, and I can't quite put my finger on it, but it's almost like they know each other. Ghost's phone buzzes again. "Just take the call," I say a little too sharply.

GHOST

Nelly looks pissed as I cancel Harriett's call for the third time and I pull her gently to one side. "You okay?"

"Why are you asking about the villa?"

"I told you earlier, I'm looking out for your parents."

"How do you know Tom? I saw how you looked at each other."

"I don't." He sighs. "Not really. I met him once."

"How?"

"Club business," I mutter.

"Don't pull that shit with me, Ghost. If it involves my parents, I want to know."

"Baby," I soothe, stroking her cheek. "Do you trust me?"

"Yes," she whispers.

"I won't let your parents be taken for fools."

She nods, and I kiss her, tipping her back slightly and putting on a show for Hugo. My phone buzzes again. "Is it Mav?" she asks.

"Harriett," I mutter.

"She clearly needs something, so answer it."

It rings off, and then Mav calls. I answer, kissing Nelly on the head and making my way outside where it's quieter. "Pres?"

"I just wanted to let you know that Harriett pressed her panic button. I've spoken to her and her ex turned up."

"She's been blowing my phone up. Is she okay?"

"We've got it. Stay with Nelly, and I'll call you when we get there."

When I go back inside, Hugo is leaning in close to Nelly, talking in her ear. Anger fills me, and as I make my way over, he tucks her hair behind her ear, his hand lingering there. I snatch it away and grip his fingers in my own, squeezing hard while lowering our hands between us so it's not obvious. He winces but does a good job of keeping a straight face. "Why are you touching my ol' lady?" I growl.

"Ghost, please," whispers Nelly, glancing around to make sure we haven't drawn attention.

"Get the message," I mutter, crushing his fingers until I feel the crunch. He hisses and his faces turns red. "Stay the fuck away from her." I release him, and he stumbles back, almost crashing into a passing waitress. "Whoops," I say, grinning and rushing to steady him as people turn to stare. "I think you've had one too many, mate," I add, patting him on the shoulder. "Careful."

He rushes off, and Nelly glares at me. "Why did you do that?"

"He was touching you," I mutter, grabbing a glass of champagne from a passing waitress and gulping it down. I cough, hating the dry taste. "Don't let him do that again."

"Or what? You'll break my fingers?" she snaps.

"No, I'd never lay a finger on you. But I'll kill him."

"That's crazy. He's nothing to me. In fact, I was just telling him how happy I was."

"And so he thought he'd touch you just to make sure you didn't feel the spark?"

"You're being ridiculous. How is Harriett?" She practically spits the words, and I roll my eyes.

"Is that what it was? You were pissed I answered a call, so you thought you'd flirt with your ex?"

"I'm not a fucking child," she snaps. "I don't play games."

"Right, of course, you don't. Yah know what, I have shit to do, so if you're gonna behave like a brat, I'll leave you to it."

"Don't let me keep you from important shit." She turns her back to me.

I shake my head. She clearly doesn't want me hanging around, so I head out. Harriett might be in a bad way, so I'll check on her and come back to get Nelly later. Hopefully, we'll both have cooled off by then.

CHAPTER THIRTEEN

NELLY

I watch him storm out and resist the urge to run after him and apologise. I don't know why I got so mad he broke Hugo's fingers, he deserved it, but I was handling Hugo myself. I was just in the process of telling him to get the fuck off me and leave me the hell alone.

I head to the bar and order a double vodka and Coke. I drink it quickly and order another. "Your parents are very lucky," comes a voice from behind me. I turn, and Tom smiles. "To be getting away from London and starting up in France."

"You'll have to show me the plans," I mutter dryly.

He pulls out his mobile phone. "I have them here," he tells me. "Let's get a drink and find a quiet booth." I watch as he flags the bartender down and proceeds to order a bottle of champagne. I hate flashy men, so it doesn't impress me, but if he wants to waste his money, I'm not about to stop him. Plus, Ghost has me worried, so I want to see these plans.

Tom leads me to a quiet booth, and I slide in opposite him. He pours the champagne and then turns his phone towards me. "So, this is what the villa will look like once it's finished," he tells me, and I stare at the beautiful, white two-story building.

"And when will that be exactly?"

"Completion should be November, weather permitting."

"Weather?" I repeat.

"Bad weather will delay building works," he explains as he flicks to the next picture. "These are the ground floor plans." It's definitely spacious. The next picture shows the second floor.

"Impressive." I drink the first glass of champagne, and he refills my glass. "Does it exist?" I ask.

His eyes flick to mine and he almost smirks. "Would you like me to get you pictures of it being built right now? I can message the builder."

"That would be great," I say. "I need the bathroom. You get those pictures."

I go to the bathroom and check myself in the mirror. I hate fighting with Ghost. It's put a dampener on the evening, and all I want to do is go home to him. I sigh heavily before fixing my hair and heading back out. I'll check these pictures and call him. I need to make things right.

Tom grins. "I've text him, just waiting on his reply."

"Great." I tip the drink back, but when he goes to refill it, I put my hand over the glass. "I'm gonna go."

"At least wait for the picture," he says.

"You could send it to me," I offer. He nods, handing me his mobile. I begin to input my number and have a moment where I can't recall my number. I frown, laughing to myself. I reach into my bag and pull out my own phone to look it up.

Tom tops up my glass while I try to figure it out. "We may as well finish it," he says, shrugging.

I hand his phone back just as it beeps. "See," he says, turning it back to me. The picture shows half the building. It really is a building site. "It's real."

My eyes feel fuzzy and I pinch the bridge of my nose. "I think I have a migraine coming," I mutter.

"Here, take a drink," he says, handing me the glass. I take a few sips and shake my head, placing it back on the table. "You don't look so good," he adds. "Have some water." He passes me an open bottle, and I down it to half.

I stand, gripping the table to steady myself. It's suddenly too hot. "Bathroom," I murmur, heading away from Tom. I crash against people as I make my way across the room before stopping at a door which I assume is the bathroom, but it's locked. "Fuck," I mutter.

"If you want the toilet, it's through that door over there," says a man from somewhere behind me. I shake my head, trying to clear it. He sounded far away, but I see another door and feel along the wall until I reach it. I push it open and stumble, landing hard on my knees.

"Fuck," I cry again, realising I'm outside and giggling to myself. Christ, I shouldn't have drank so quickly—it's hit me hard all of a sudden and I can't see straight. Standing on shaky legs, I hold on to the opposite wall to steady myself, and when I turn, I see the door is now closed. "No!" I wail, rushing back to it. It looks like a fire exit, and there's no handle, although it's hard to tell with blurred vision. I try and prize my fingers along the edge, but it won't budge. "Great."

I lean against the wall and open my bag, feeling around inside for my phone. I need to speak to Ghost, but my hands don't feel like they're gripping right, almost like they're not attached to my body, and the contents of my bag spill out, scattering across the alley. I groan aloud when I spot my phone, now in separate pieces.

"Let me help with that." A man appears, and I try to focus my eyes on him, but they're blurry, making him look fuzzy and dream-like. "I'm not sure if you've fucked your phone up," he says, tapping it. "Yep, it's broken." He then drops it, crunching it under his foot. I frown in confusion. "Oops," he murmurs.

"Wh-...yo-..." My words sound odd. Everything begins spinning and I grab the wall for safety.

"Come on, baby, let me take care of you," whispers a voice, and I smile. Ghost is here. He must have come back for me. I'm being lifted into his arms. I can't control my head, so I rest it on his chest. He doesn't smell the same. He takes a few steps, and then I'm placed on the ground. It's cold, but my arms are heavy and nothing seems to be working right. "I saw your pictures, but they didn't do you justice, baby," he mutters in my ear.

"Gho- . . . Gho- . . ." Am I saying it right? It doesn't feel right. My voice is slow, and I try again to focus my eyes, but each time I open them, it makes me feel sick. Why is everything moving so fast?

"I'm here, beautiful. Relax."

Beautiful. Since when does he call me that? I smirk . . . at least, I think I do. Why is it cold? My mouth is so dry that my tongue feels swollen. That must be why I can't talk. I don't remember ever feeling like this, and I try hard to recall the drinks I had tonight, but it all seems like so much effort. "You look good in the dress, baby," the voice whispers. It sounds distorted now, like a robot. Then something is placed over my face, but I can't turn my head to get it off. Is it my dress? Maybe that's why I'm cold.

I focus hard on trying to turn my head away from the material, and my brain is screaming for me to move, but my limbs aren't listening. It's no good, it's all too heavy and I can't move anything. Then, I feel an intrusion between my legs, a pressure at my opening. Where the hell is my underwear?

Something's not right. Why does it hurt like that? I want to scream, the pain is so excruciating. I try to speak. Ghost needs to know I'm not feeling well and he's hurting me, but the words won't come out at all now. I can't make a sound. I try desperately to move my hands, but even my fingers feel different. Something's banging against my head. A wall? *Thud, thud, thud.* I don't know how long it is before the thudding stops, but it seems like a long time. Words drift in and out. I don't know who's saying them, but they sound ugly. I don't like these words.

The pain goes and the material slips from my face. A kiss is pressed to my mouth, but it's not gentle. Ghost is always gentle. His tongue feels too wet, and I know I'm not kissing him back, so why isn't he checking I'm okay? Why isn't he checking on me like he always does?

Then, suddenly, I'm in a park. I blink in confusion. Lucy is sitting on the park bench. She waves to me, but there are tears running down her cheeks. Why is she so sad? Luce? I reach out my hand, but it doesn't quite touch her, and I can't shout to her because nothing's working.

Nothing works.

GHOST

I pace the corridor of the hospital with rage pulsing through my veins. "I'll fucking kill him," I growl, squeezing my fists open and closed.

"Cambridge just booked on a flight," Grim cuts in, looking up from his laptop.

"Great, let's go," I snap, heading for the exit.

Mav steps in front of me, shaking his head. "Brother, we can't go after him. The cops have already been called."

"I'll do time, I don't care," I snap.

"What about Nelly?" The mention of her makes me stop. "She needs you, brother, relax. We'll get Cambridge in our own time. The main thing is that Harriett is okay."

"She's a fucking mess," I spit. "How the hell did this happen again?"

"He'd been served with the restraining order and he's been quiet since. No one could have foreseen this," mutters Hadley.

"Where's Nelly?" asks Rosey.

"She's with her parents," I mutter. The anger I felt at her earlier has disappeared. Seeing Harriett all beat up made me want to hold on to Nelly even tighter. I pull out my phone to call her, maybe she's finished at the party and needs a ride. It goes straight to voicemail. "Listen, baby," I say into the phone, "I'm sorry, okay. I fucked up. Harriett is in a bad way. Her ex beat her pretty badly. Nelly, I need you. Please call me when you need a ride and I'll come get you." I disconnect just as the doctor comes out of Harriett's room.

"She's asking for Ghost," says the doctor. I nod before following him into the room.

Harriett is sitting up with cuts and bruises to her face, but she manages a smile when she sees me. I grab her hands in mine and rest my forehead against hers. "I am so sorry I didn't pick up," I mutter.

"It's fine. I didn't realise you were at Nelly's parents' party. Rylee told me."

"Are you okay?"

"I've had worse," she jokes, but neither of us laugh.

"You're moving in to the club," I tell her. "No arguments. You've become like a sister to me, H, and I can't bear the thought of that shit bag coming back and killing you, cos that's how this is gonna end if you don't let us help you."

She nods reluctantly. "Thanks."

We hang around the hospital until visiting hours are over and the doctor kicks us out. I head back to the party to see if Nelly needs a ride, but she hasn't called. It's almost midnight, so I'm pretty sure she'll be ready to leave.

Inside, I spot Charlotte and head over. "Is Nelly still here?" I ask.

She laughs. "The last time I saw her, she was stumbling her way towards the bathroom. I think she'd had too much champagne. I sent Hugo to check on her and maybe put her in a cab."

I nod, adrenaline pumping through me at the thought of Hugo being alone with her. I look around the busy room, but I can't see her, so I head for the bathroom and bang on the door. "Nelly, are you in there?"

A female steps out. "There's no one else in there," she tells me.

I try calling again, but again, it goes to voicemail. Maybe she's already made her way home.

NELLY

My head is thumping. I peel my eyes open and blink, but they feel like they're full of sand. Lifting my hand to rub them, it's shaking so bad, I have trouble guiding it to where I need it. "Morning, Sleeping Beauty," murmurs a man's voice from beside me. I stare in horror at Tom, who's lying beside me in a bed I don't know. "Bet you've got the hangover from hell."

My heart beats faster as I look around. It looks like a hotel room. "Where am I?" I ask, my voice is croaky and my mouth is dry.

"Here, have a drink," he says, reaching to the table beside him and grabbing a bottle of water. He unscrews the cap and hands it to me. I sit slowly, but my body feels stiff and achy, like I've done a hard training session with Grim in the gym, and I struggle to take the bottle. As I do, the sheet falls from my chest and I stare down at my naked breasts. I immediately pull the sheet back in place, and Tom grins, cupping my breast and tweaking my nipple. "You weren't so shy last night, beautiful." I shudder at that word. I have a vague memory of him whispering that to me. "Hugo said you loved cock, but Christ, I wasn't expecting you to be so fucking horny."

"We had sex?" I ask, because honestly, I don't remember a thing.

He pulls me back towards him and wraps his arm around my neck, as his other hand pulls the sheet away and he runs it down my front. I twist away, clamping my legs shut before his hand can touch me there. "You wanna fight?" he asks, cocking his eyebrow and grinning.

"I have a boyfriend," I say, trying hard to stop the tears that are waiting to fall. I couldn't have cheated. I wouldn't.

Tom takes the bottle from me and places it back on the side. "You didn't give a crap about him when you were coming all over my cock," he says, leaning down to take my nipple in his mouth. I push his head away, and he looks at me in surprise. "What's wrong?"

"Get off me," I snap. I'm suddenly aware I'm alone in a hotel room with a man I don't know.

"Are you being serious?" he asks, looking confused.

"Deadly."

He releases me. "Fine, but don't come at me just because you cheated on your boyfriend."

"I didn't cheat. I'd never do that to him."

Tom laughs and gets up from the bed. He's naked, his erection standing proud, and I turn away, my stomach in knots. I feel sick. I try desperately to remember what happened, but everything seems so hazy. The last clear memory I have is going to the bathroom and making the decision to call Ghost.

Tom begins pulling on his clothes. "It was great and all that, but I have a wife and she's a little crazy when it comes to other women. It's probably best we don't have contact again."

"Did we . . . erm, did we use protection?" I feel embarrassed that I don't already know the answer.

Tom grins. "Of course. I don't want no kids. I wrapped it all three times," he says.

"Three?"

He laughs. "You really don't remember?" I shake my head. "You begged me to get a room here."

"And you didn't think I was too . . . drunk?"

He scowls. "Hey, don't start that bullshit. You came onto me. You fucked me. Bitch, you were riding me like a fucking rodeo bull and you enjoyed every minute. I've never seen any woman orgasm like that." Sickness builds again and I bite my lower lip as tears slip down my cheeks. Ghost is gonna hate me. Tom sighs and sits beside me on the bed. I suddenly feel vulnerable that he's seen me naked and he's touched me intimately. Touched me in ways only Ghost touches me. I shift away from him when he runs a finger over my bare shoulder. "Look, don't be too hard on yourself. We all fuck up at some point. The trick is, don't tell anyone."

"I have to tell him," I mutter, burying my head in my hands.

"I'm not going to, so you really don't have to."

"Where's my stuff?" I ask.

"You broke your phone, but the rest of your things are on the chair," he says, standing. "I'll leave you to get dressed. Take care, beautiful." He leaves the room, and the second the door closes, I burst into tears. I can't believe I fucked it all up.

GHOST

I've spent the entire night riding around London, combing the streets for Nelly, who isn't receiving my calls and is nowhere to be found. Mav calls me to check in and informs me none of the other guys have had any luck either. "Maybe we should call the cops," I suggest.

"You know they're not gonna do anything for at least forty-eight hours," he says.

"It's not like her, Mav. I'm really worried."

There's a commotion on his end of the phone. "Fuck, she's just walked in, Ghost. Get back here."

The ride back to the club seems like the longest ever. I'm so relieved she's safe that when I burst in and see her with the women, I pull her hard against me and breathe in her scent. She doesn't really hug me back, so I hold her at arm's length and do a quick assessment. She isn't meeting my eyes, so I assume she's still mad with me over our argument last night. "I've been worried sick," I tell her.

"Sorry. I got drunk and passed out."

"I've been calling you. I went by your place. I've spent the night looking for you."

"Sorry," she mumbles again.

I frown at her weird behaviour. "The guys have been up all night," I continue, needing her to see how worried we've all been.

"I said sorry, Ghost. What do you want me to do?"

"What happened to your phone? I got your voicemail all night."

"I dropped it. It smashed."

"Right, and you didn't think to find a pay phone? Where did you sleep?"

"What's with the questions? I got a room in a hotel. Can I just go and sleep off this hangover?" she snaps.

Rylee places her hand against my chest and shakes her head, indicating I should leave it. Rosey takes Nelly and leads her upstairs. "What the hell?" I mutter.

"She's tired and hungover," says Rylee gently. "Let her sleep it off and she'll be fine. You can get your answers then."

CHAPTER FOURTEEN

NELLY

"Is everything okay?" asks Rosey, following me into the bedroom.

"Yeah," I mutter.

"Cos you're acting odd. And you have a lost look in your eyes."

"Do I?"

"Where were you last night, Nelly? We were all really worried."

I begin to cry again, unable to keep it all inside. "Rosey, I think I did something really, really bad."

"Like broke the law bad?" she asks, looking concerned.

"Like fucked my life bad," I sob.

"Oh god, Nelly, you didn't cheat on him?" she groans.

I nod, crying into my hands. "And I don't remember it. I just woke up and there he was."

"Who?"

"A guy my parents know. He's married," I wail. "Ghost is gonna hate me."

"You need to tell me everything," she says, dragging me to sit beside her on the bed.

"But I don't remember any of it. I remember talking to him, and the next thing, we're in bed waking up beside each other naked."

"Were you drunk?"

I shrug. "I had maybe five drinks. I drank them fast, but I don't feel it was enough to make me forget the night. It feels like a fuzzy memory."

"Nelly, what if he drugged you?"

I stare at her, letting her words process. "Would he have hung around until I woke up if he did? He'd surely be out of there first thing."

"Not necessarily. Not if he wanted you to think you'd consented."

I shake my head. "No, he was acting normal. I don't think that's what happened, and honestly, it sounds like something I'd do."

"Maybe we should get Doc to run a blood test to be sure."

"No," I snap. "No. I need to sleep. I don't feel too good."

"Shaky?" she asks, and I nod. "Headache?" I nod again. "If you leave it too long, whatever he gave you could be out your system by the time you get checked. All your symptoms are pointing to being drugged."

My heart squeezes. "They're pointing to a hangover."

"I think we should talk to Ghost."

"No," I snap. "No way. I need to figure it all out before I talk to him."

"Figure what? He's been out of his mind with worry. What are you gonna tell him?"

"The truth," I mutter. "The truth. But I need to sleep off this hangover first. Maybe I can beg him to forgive me, explain I was drunk." I lay down, and Rosey smiles at me sadly. "You don't think he will?" I ask, pulling the sheet around me. She shakes her head, gently rubbing my arm. "Me either," I admit, closing my eyes. I feel too sick to face any of it right now.

GHOST

I hold the pregnancy test kit in my hand and watch Nelly sleeping. She's restless, moaning and crying out like she's having nightmares. I check my watch. It's eight in the evening, and she's slept the whole day. I need to talk to her about where she disappeared to and why she didn't tell me she'd brought a pregnancy test. I'd found it tucked away in her drawer when I was searching for her address book last night.

Placing my arm around her waist, I tuck my nose into her hair. She doesn't smell of her usual mango shampoo. "Baby," I whisper. She starts, stiffening in fright before pushing me away. I stare at her in alarm. "It's just me."

She's panting like she's run a marathon. "Shit, you scared me. What time is it?"

"It's eight in the evening. You slept all day."

She shivers, wrapping the sheets around her. "I don't feel good."

"You don't look good, baby. Do you want me to call Doc?" She shakes her head but closes her eyes. "When did you get these?" I ask, and she opens one eye to see the pregnancy kit.

"Why were you going through my things?"

"I was looking for your address book to see if I could call your friends last night when I was going out of my mind."

"I don't know half those old friends now. My friends are here at the club."

"I was desperate," I admit, and she looks guilty for a second. "Do you think you're pregnant?"

"My period is a couple of days late. It was just a precaution. No big deal."

"But you drank." I don't mean it to sound so accusing, but it does, and she scowls.

"I had a few drinks. I don't even think I'm pregnant. I'm late all the time."

"Let's do the test and see. It could explain why your hangover is so bad," I say, opening the box. "It can't hurt to check."

"Will you let me sleep if I do it?" she asks.

I nod, handing her the test. "Deal."

NELLY

I feel so dizzy, it's hard to stay upright, but I make it to the bathroom and pee onto the stick. I really only got the tests for future use. There's no way I can be pregnant already, although we have had a lot of sex. I think about Tom again and shudder. I hate myself for what I've done and I'll need to get the morning after pill to ensure I don't get pregnant because he could have lied about using protection. I pop the cap on the test and lay it on the side unit. The first line appears to show the test is working, so I head back to bed, confident it will be negative.

"Where were you last night?" asks Ghost, watching me closely.

"I told you."

"Which hotel?"

"Ghost, please. My head hurts and I feel terrible. It's not a big deal. We had a fight, and I needed time alone."

"So, why didn't you go to your place?"

"Because you'd have found me and made me come back here. Look, I should have called, I'm sorry, but I was drunk, and it's a shit excuse, but I can't do anything about it now. I'm really sorry."

"Was Hugo with you?" he asks stiffly.

"No, Ghost. Please, let me sleep."

He nods once and goes into the bathroom. "Don't do that again, okay. I can give you space, but don't disappear like that."

"I won't."

"And the drinking needs to stop," he adds.

I frown. "Okay, but I really don't drink often, and—"

"I mean because of this," he says, standing in the doorway and holding up the test. "Because you're gonna have my kid."

I go into shock . . . completely frozen, unable to speak shock. I close my eyes for the briefest minute and I'm suddenly transported somewhere else. I feel cold, and I hear heavy breaths, like panting in my ear. *"Beautiful."* I shiver and my eyes spring open. Ghost is watching me with concern. "Are you okay?" he asks, and I nod. "Baby, we're gonna be parents," he says, a smile breaking out on his face. He rushes over and scoops me up against him. "We're gonna have a baby." I'm still too stunned to respond, and I have a terrible feeling in my stomach. Something bad happened to me last night, and now, I'll have to face up to it.

Ghost lets me sleep the rest of the night, and when he wakes me the next morning, it's with a tray of eggs and bacon. My stomach recoils, but I force a smile and take the tray. "I booked you in with Doc.

He's gonna do another test and make it all official," says Ghost excitedly. I want to be excited too, but I know once I tell him the truth about where I was, things are going to go very wrong. What if I end up a single parent? I never wanted that for my kids, but I guess no parent ever wants that.

Once I'm dressed, I go downstairs where Ghost is waiting for me. Rosey intercepts me, pulling me to one side. "How are you?"

I force a smile again, which is becoming a habit. "Great. You?"

She gives me a look that tells me she isn't buying my bull. "No, really, how are you?"

I feel tears filling my already sore eyes and I blink them away. "Not now, Rosey. Ghost's waiting to take me to the doctor."

She smiles. "Great, you decided to go then? Did you tell him?"

"No," I hiss. "It's for something else. Look, I really have to go."

Ghost grabs my hand and leads the way out to his bike. "Let's get this confirmed and then we'll make the announcement."

"We should wait, with my history. At least until the twelve-week mark."

"Baby, this is our family. They've got our backs, and they'll be so happy. Plus, they can keep an eye on you and make sure you're resting, I know what you're like for pushing yourself too hard."

Ghost is holding my hand so tight, I can't help smiling up at him as we watch the blurry image of a bean on the sonographer's screen. "There's the heartbeat. It's strong," she says, pointing to a black space where a tiny flicker beats. "You're nine weeks," she adds.

I'm surprised. I never expected to catch at all, so to hear I'm so far gone is a relief. "And everything looks okay?" Ghost asks.

"So far, so good," she says, smiling. She presses a button and prints off some pictures. "I'd like you back here in three weeks so we can get some measurements. By then, you'll be twelve weeks, and we'll hopefully be out of the risky period."

As we step from the room, the club's doctor—ironically, they call him Doc—is passing. "Actually, can I have a quick word?" I ask, letting go of Ghost's hand. "Can you wait outside for me?" I add to Ghost.

"What do you wanna ask that I can't know?" He looks confused.

"Girl stuff," I say, adding a smile. "I'll be a minute."

He reluctantly walks out, and I take a nervous breath to calm myself. "Random question, but if a woman was drugged, how would she know?"

Doc frowns, glancing out the window to where Ghost is leaning against the wall and looking at his phone. "Drugged in what way?"

I swallow the lump in my throat. "I dunno . . . say, something was put in her drink?"

"Well, there are signs. Loss of memory, thumping headache, sore limbs."

I mentally tick them off in my head. "Right. And what would she need to do to get proof it actually happened?"

He shifts uncomfortably. "Nelly, are you okay?"

I smile. "Yes, it's not me. A woman I'm working with at the centre thinks it happened on a night out."

He relaxes slightly. "Okay, well, she'd need to go to a doctor and get blood tests. But there's a time limit. In blood, it would show up to twenty-four hours. Or she can get a urine test, and that can show the drug up to maybe seventy-two hours. The sooner she sees a medical professional, the better, because it varies from person to person." I nod. "And Nelly, she should also get checked out. Usually in cases where a person has been drugged through drink on a night out, it ends in something more serious."

I nod again. "Okay. I'll tell her."

"Even if she doesn't want to do anything right now, it's better to get seen and have it all on record so she can make important decisions once she's feeling able to face it."

GHOST

Nelly seems distant. When she steps from Doc's, I grab her and push her gently against the wall. "I fucking love you," I say, kissing her. It takes me a second to realise she's not kissing me back. "You okay?"

"I need to talk to you," she mutters. My phone rings and I groan, releasing her and checking the caller ID.

"It's Harriett. Hold that thought," I say, connecting the call. "Hey."

"I can come home," she tells me.

"Right. Let me drop Nelly home and I'll come get you."

I disconnect, and Nelly squeezes my hand. "Actually, you go get her now. I need a walk. I'm still not feeling one hundred percent, and the fresh air will do me good."

I glance around. "I'd prefer to drop you off."

"It's fine. Harriett needs you. Go."

I watch her walk away and my gut twists. Something's wrong, but I can't put my finger on it. Part of me is worried this has something to do with Hugo, and that's the part that's stopping me from really pushing her for answers.

Harriett is waiting in the reception when I arrive at the hospital. "Is Ivy okay?" she asks me.

"Absolutely fine. Mama B and Diamond are spoiling her."

She visibly relaxes. "Good. I can't wait to see her." I grab her hand and lead her from the hospital. People stare as we pass, and I know they think I've done this to her. People are so quick to judge my appearance. "Meli opened your shop today," I tell her, trying to distract her from the whispering and judgemental stares. "She's happy to take over until you're feeling better."

"I'm sorry," she whispers behind me.

I stop and turn to face her. "For what?"

"All these people think you've done this to me," she mutters, her eyes watering.

I brush a finger over her bruised cheek. "We know the truth, and that's all that matters."

We get back to the club and Nelly still isn't back. My heart immediately speeds up until Mav confirms Rosey went to meet her for a walk. Maybe a chat with Rosey will bring her out of this strange mood.

Church is called and I take my seat at the table next to Scar. "You okay?" I ask, and he nods.

"D-did she s-say where she went to?" he asks.

"Not really. Just that she crashed in a hotel."

"A-and you're happy w-with that?"

I shrug. "Not really, but what can I do now? Besides, we got distracted," I tell him, keeping my voice low. I pull out the strip of pictures the sonographer gave us. Scar snatches them and grins. "So, I didn't want to argue with her and stress her out."

"Shit, is that what I think it is?" asks Mav, peering over Scar's shoulder. The other guys quiet down to see what we're looking at.

"I wanted to announce it properly," I say, laughing. "But now I have your attention, Nelly and I are having a baby."

Cheers erupt around the room and I'm congratulated over and over. It feels good to have everyone as excited as I am, especially when Nelly doesn't seem so thrilled. Dad pulls me in for a hug. "I'm so proud of you, Eric," he says close to my ear. "Your mum is gonna be thrilled."

Later, when Nelly returns with Rosey, she looks tired, but Mav doesn't give her a chance to escape. Instead, he grabs her by the hand and pulls her to the front of the main room to get everyone's attention. I join them, taking her other hand. "I just want to take a second to congratulate Ghost and his fine lady, Nelly. They're gonna have a baby!"

Dad was right because Mum practically screams in delight and throws herself at us for a group hug. Nelly catches me watching her over Mum's shoulder and gives a small smile that doesn't quite reach her eyes. That bad gut feeling returns, but I push it away. Joining the brothers by the bar, I leave the women to sweep Nelly up in the excitement they're clearly feeling more than she is. Maybe they'll rub off on her.

A few hours pass and I spot her yawning, so I go over and pull her to stand. "Early night?" I ask. It's the longest we've gone without sex, and I can't wait to get her alone. Being distant from each other is making me think crazy thoughts. I just need us to feel close again.

I go for a shower, and when I return to the bedroom, Nelly is tucked up with her eyes closed. I smile. No way is she getting out of this, so I slip under the sheet and snuggle up behind her. She doesn't respond as I run my hand up her thigh and across her stomach to cup her breast. "I missed you," I whisper into her hair. I push my erection against her arse and feel her stiffen.

NELLY

I try to ignore Ghost as he gropes at my body. Squeezing my eyes shut, I wonder why the hell I'm repulsed by his touch. "Didn't you wanna tell me something?" he asks as he places small kisses against my neck.

After speaking with Rosey, she convinced me to hold off telling Ghost anything until I was sure either way. I gave her a pee sample, which she took to a doctor friend with no connection to the club. "It can wait," I whisper.

"You don't seem yourself," he adds, pushing up my nightshirt and rolling me onto my back.

"I'm just tired," I mutter, running my fingers through his hair.

He moves down my body, taking a nipple in his mouth and humming his approval. I close my eyes again and concentrate on Ghost. My Ghost. The man I love. The soon to be father of my child.

"You're so fucking beautiful," he whispers, kissing down my stomach as he moves lower. I cringe at his words and repeat Ghost's name in my head. His hands cup my arse and he lifts me slightly to his mouth. "I've missed your taste," he growls, licking the length of my opening.

My entire body locks up. I freeze and, suddenly, it's like I'm not in the room anymore. Instead, I'm somewhere cold and dark. I can hear people talking in the distance, like they're nearby but not close enough to help me. And I need help. I know I need it, but I can't shout for it. There's pain between my legs and a heavy feeling on my chest. There's panting, deep groans of ecstasy, but they're not coming from me and I don't recognise the owner of them. Those sounds aren't Ghost. And then there's a thudding. It's me, thudding up against something as thrusts hit my pelvis and my head bangs on something above me. Maybe a wall?

Thud thud thud. Pant pant pant. "*You're a fucking whore. Hugo told me.*" *Thud thud thud. There's laughter nearby, and I imagine it's a group of friends heading home for the night. I'm cold, so fucking cold, and my back hurts with the weight on top of me, crushing me with each push forward.*

"Nelly! Nelly! Jesus, what the fuck are you doing?" I blink and the room comes back into focus. There's a sobbing sound and I realise it's me and my chest is heaving in time with my sobs. Ghost is sitting up between my open legs and staring at me in shock. "What's wrong?"

I can't catch my breath to explain, so he pulls my nightshirt into place and settles beside me. He tugs me against his chest and holds me while I cry. We must lay like that for ten minutes, until my tears have run down his stomach, making it wet and slippy. I sniffle a few more times, then use the sheet to wipe him. "I know the hormones are supposed to send you crazy, but man, I did not expect that," says Ghost playfully.

"Sorry," I whisper.

"Don't be sorry, baby. It's not your fault."

"It is. I . . . I . . ."

"Nelly, listen to me, it's just hormones. You can cry, scream, whatever you need to do. I'm gonna be here to scoop you up and hold you until it passes. Now, sleep. You're exhausted. I love you."

I smile gratefully at my wonderful man. "I love you too."

CHAPTER FIFTEEN

GHOST

Church the following morning is charged with energy. It's been a while since we needed to call on our darker side, but knowing we're about to confront that piece of shit who's about to rip off Nelly's parents gives me a smug satisfaction. We've done our checks, and with Arthur's help, we discovered that Tom Prescott sells fake properties to people wanting to make their dreams come true. I'm still trying to find out if Hugo has anything to do with it seeing as he introduced them.

Mav goes over the plan one last time and then I head out alongside him, Grim, and Scar.

When we enter Tom Prescott's office, he smiles with a relaxed demeanor. "Boys, I take it you're here for the next instalment?" he asks.

"I take it you're gonna give us another excuse," I reply, closing the door and locking it.

Grim closes the window blinds, and I finally see a flicker of fear in Prescott's eyes. There's something about the fear in a man's eyes that gives me peace and I take a deep, relaxing breath. "We're not here on behalf of Arthur Taylor," I tell him, taking a seat opposite him.

"He's coming for you himself to settle that score," adds Mav.

"I can pay him. I have the first payment," Prescott splutters.

"It's about time you started to sound worried," I say. "You really didn't do your research when you decided to borrow money from the Taylors. You won't get away with months of missed payments."

"I have nothing he can take," Prescott spits angrily.

I nod in agreement. "We know. We looked into you. But I have to say, you're good, and we were quite impressed."

"I can be useful," he says, his tone begging. "I can get new identities, passports, whatever you need."

"And I'm sure the Taylors will take full advantage of those skills. But we're not here about your fake identity or your bullshit life," says Mav.

"The half-a-million-pound villa project," I begin, and Prescott pales. "We had a friend look into it." I pull out an envelope and lay it on his desk. "Look inside," I tell him.

He grabs the envelope with a shaky hand and pulls out the photographs inside. "Lay them out," Grim tells him, and he does. The bare wasteland stares back at us.

"This is the plot you're selling to my in-laws," I say, "but it's not quite what they think."

"I can explain," he rushes to tell me. "It's taken time to get off the ground. The first contractors pulled out and—" I slam my hands on the desk, and he stops talking.

"You're a conman, Tom, or should I say Elliot Smith. Now, I know they've given you quite a deposit and I'll be needing that back."

He shakes his head. "I don't have it."

"You haven't been paying the contractors or the Taylors for their loan, so where is it?"

"I have debts. Lots of them," he mutters.

"Not my problem," I snap.

"I need time."

"Unfortunately, you don't have that either," I tell him.

Grim hits him hard, and his head snaps back. His nose busts and blood floods out onto his shirt. "We've put a guy on you, to make sure you don't skip the country or do anything silly," I tell him. "I'm giving you time to shift your assets around because we know about your wife and her inheritance. We know you have access to money. We also know about your many identities, so it won't take us long to find the money should we need to start looking. So, get resourceful, and we'll pop back soon."

The clubhouse is empty when we get back. Rylee arranged a fun day at her women's centre up the road and everyone was going to help out. We park our bikes at the club and walk up to find the place packed out. I spot Nelly behind the desk chatting with some women and she looks her usual happy self. I catch her eye and smile, and then join Scar, who is holding his ol' lady, Gracie, to his side. "How does it feel?" asks Gracie.

"Fucking good," I tell her, grinning.

"I'm really pleased for you, Ghost. Nelly is fantastic."

I nod in agreement. "She doesn't seem happy about the baby," I blurt out, desperate to get the thought out my head.

"She's probably just adjusting to the news," Gracie explains. "It's huge."

I nod, but I don't feel any better. "She lost a baby before and then thought she couldn't have them."

"Then that's your answer, she's nervous the same will happen. You just have to look after her and reassure her she'll be okay."

NELLY

It's exhausting pretending to be okay when I keep getting flashbacks of the other night. If they're real, then Rosey could be right. I don't think I consented to sex with Tom, and I don't know how to feel about that, so I've pushed it down. I'm trying hard not to think about it right now because this day is so important to the centre and to Rylee.

I manage to avoid Rosey and Ghost for most of the day, and it's only as the visitors begin to leave and it quiets down that I realise I need to get answers from Rosey.

I find her outside on the grass with her head tipped back and her eyes closed. "Hey," I whisper, and she jumps in fright.

"My skills are disappearing," she complains as I lower to sit beside her. "Since coming back here, they're slowly going. I used to be able to hear the drop of a pin and now I've got fully grown adults sneaking up on me."

"Did you speak to your doctor?"

She nods, biting her lip. "There was nothing, Nelly."

My stomach lurches and tears immediately pool in my eyes. "Really?" I'd finally convinced myself that maybe I didn't cheat, and I can't handle knowing that I did all over again.

"He did say that it could have left your system. It depends what drug was used and the amount. I think we left it too late."

Tears trickle down my cheeks. "So, I cheated."

"No, Nelly, you didn't. You know deep down you didn't consent. You weren't in any fit state to."

I shake my head and swipe away my tears. "I have no proof of that. Stop trying to make excuses. I'm a dirty cheat and I'm gonna break Ghost's heart."

Rosie grabs my hands. "You don't have to. He doesn't need to know."

"Don't be ridiculous. The guilt is eating me up inside. I'm even imagining I was rap—" I suck in a shaky breath, unable to say the word out loud. "I have to be honest."

A woman approaches, glaring down at me. "Hey, can I help?" I ask, wiping my cheeks and pushing to stand. "I'm Nelly."

I don't see the slap until it's too late. My cheek stings and I gasp in shock. "I know who you are," she hisses.

Rosey stands. "What the fuck are you doing," she yells.

"This dirty little slag had sex with my husband," the woman screams.

Ghost rushes over, pulling me behind him. "What the fuck are you doing, lady?" he growls.

"Are you the boyfriend?" the woman asks, arching her brows.

"Who the fuck are you?" snaps Rosey.

"Your cheap whore of a girlfriend slept with my husband on Saturday night," the woman spits. "I should rip her fucking hair out!"

Ghost turns to look at me. "What is she talking about?" he asks, and I know he's connecting the dots. Sickness bubbles in my chest and tears free fall down my cheeks and onto my top.

"It's not how it seems," says Rosey.

"You know about this?" yells Ghost, taking a step back from us both and standing beside the woman.

"A cheap hotel for a cheap fuck," snaps the woman, producing a key card from the hotel. "He didn't pay, of course. No, I got the courtesy when they called me to chase payment."

I'm crying so hard, my chest aches, and I bend slightly, resting my hands on my knees and trying desperately to suck air into my lungs. "Is this true?" asks Ghost. "That's where you were on Saturday when I was out looking for you?"

"No, Ghost, it wasn't like that," Rosey tries again. I grab her hand, and she looks at me. I shake my head because she can't lie on my behalf. As much as she wants to believe I was drugged, it's not the truth

"I'm so sorry," I sniffle. "I was really drunk and I—"

Ghost grabs my upper arm, pulling me close. Rosey begins yelling and trying to pull us apart, but she's not strong enough. He pushes his face into mine. "Look me in the eyes and tell me you cheated," he says in a low, angry voice.

I swallow the lump in my throat and nod. "I cheated," I tell him. "I cheated. I'm so sorry."

"Let her go, Ghost," screams Rosey, trying to force herself between us, but he grips me tighter.

"With who?"

"It doesn't matter," I mutter, wincing when he squeezes harder.

The brothers are all around us, yelling at Ghost to let me go, but we're locked in some kind of staring contest. "I'm gonna find out from his wife anyway, so I want his name."

"Don't say his name, Nelly," yells Mav. "For fuck's sake, don't say his name."

"Tell me," Ghost growls. I shake my head, but his other hand cups the back of my head and he presses his forehead against mine. "Nelly, so help me, God, I'll do something I'll regret if you don't give me his name."

The shouting fades out and that voice is in my ear hissing words of hate. *Slag. Whore. Dirty bitch.* I shake my head to make it stop. "Is it even my kid?" Ghost snaps.

I nod. "Yes."

"Like I can believe you now. How could you do this to me, to us?" he yells, releasing me and pushing me from him like I'm a dirty dog hanging onto him.

The woman is gone and so is Mav. He must have taken her so Ghost couldn't get a name. Rosey stands between me and Ghost, and he laughs. "You think you can stop me?" he asks her. He's lashing out because he wants a fight.

"Try me," says Rosey coldly. "I eat boys like you for breakfast."

"I bet you do. So does my ol' lady apparently." He brings his eyes to me and they're full of hate. "I could have given you everything, Nelly."

I watch through blurred vision as he walks away. August appears from beside Scar and pushes her hands hard against my shoulders. I stumble back, falling to the ground. "You dirty whore." She spits at my feet and runs after her uncle.

The bystanders disperse. The brothers go after Ghost to keep him calm while Rosey holds out her hand to help me up. The other ol' ladies stand around, unsure what to do. Rylee tells everyone to go back to the club, then leads me and Rosey into the centre, which is now quiet. She locks us inside and we go into one of the meeting rooms.

"Start from the beginning," she says.

GHOST

"Brother, you need a clear head," says Grim, watching as I drink from the bottle of vodka. I gulp until it's a quarter gone. "It's not gonna help."

"Really, VP?" I ask. "Cos it feels like it is."

"He's right," says Dad.

"Sleep it off," suggests Mum.

"Sleep it off? My ol' lady cheated on me!"

"Things will seem brighter once you've slept on it," she says.

"I'm fine. I just need some peace," I mutter, drinking more from the bottle. Mav ushers everyone away. "Who was that woman?"

"I didn't bother getting her name, brother. I sent her away and told her not to return here."

"Wouldn't you wanna know?" I snap.

"Of course, man, but I know what you'll do when you find out and I don't wanna see you inside. Whatever's happened, Nelly is carrying your kid, and you can't go to prison."

"If it is my kid," I mutter bitterly.

"Brother, this is Nelly we're talking about. She's a good person. Let's wait and see what Rylee comes back with. She's with her now."

"Pres, she told me. She said it to my face. She cheated. There's no coming back from that. We're over."

"There might be a really good explanation," he suggests doubtfully.

"What, she slipped and fell on his dick?" I ask, smirking. "What would you do if it was Rylee?"

Mav thinks for a second. "I dunno, man. I honestly don't know. I'd be raging, obviously, but I love her so damn much, I don't know if I could let her go." He shrugs. "But I guess being around her once the trust is gone would make me toxic. It probably wouldn't work."

"Exactly," I mutter, swigging a few more mouthfuls. "The way I feel right now, I wanna kill them both."

Mav sits beside me. "Then I'll stick beside you until it passes cos I ain't losing my brother to prison."

Scar joins us, patting me on the back and sliding an empty glass my way for a fill. "I h-had to d-deal with August," he explains. "Sh-she got herself all t-twisted over Nelly."

"Yeah?"

"Sh-she p-pushed her."

I grimace, knowing Nelly is pregnant. "Is August okay?" I ask, standing.

"Yeah, she's good."

"I gotta check Nelly," I mutter.

"You gonna stay calm?" asks Mav. I nod. "Okay, we'll come too."

The centre is locked. Mav produces a key, and the minute the door is open, I march in, opening doors until I find her. All three women look around in surprise, and it's obvious they've been crying. I take Nelly's hand and tug her to stand. She does, keeping her eyes lowered. I run my thumb over the bruise I put on her forearm and feel sick to my stomach. "I'm sorry," I say.

"It's fine," she whispers, still keeping her eyes lowered.

"It's not fine. I shouldn't have grabbed you. I'm a dick. Scar said August pushed you." She nods. "Are you okay? Is the baby okay?" She nods again. "Maybe we should get you checked?"

"I'm fine. The baby is fine."

I release her hand and it drops to her side. "I'll have your stuff moved out to a spare room," I tell her, and she stiffens. "I can't be around you right now," I add, explaining, "but we'll talk. There's things we need to discuss, like the baby and shit."

"And us?" she asks, bringing her eyes to meet mine.

The tug on my heart seeing her so sad breaks me. I step towards the door, looking away and putting distance between us. "We're done, Nelly. There isn't an us anymore."

CHAPTER SIXTEEN

NELLY

"You have to tell Ghost about this," says Rylee gently. "You're in denial, but I honestly think Rosey is on to something here. Even if he didn't drug you, you certainly didn't consent. It doesn't sound like you gave him any signal other than you wanted to leave. He insisted you drink the champagne. I think you should go and get examined. Doctors can tell if there's signs of trauma."

I'm already shaking my head. "I had sex with another man. I cheated. There's no excuse. I shouldn't have gotten drunk, and I shouldn't have accepted a drink from a stranger. This is my fault."

"Oh, Nelly. It's not. I promise it isn't your fault. If we told Ghost he—"

"No!" I snap. "We're not telling Ghost. You're giving him false hope if you make him think I could have been attacked. Because all the tests could come back normal, and then he's just got to go through the pain again of realising what I've done. This is between us, and I'm begging you to keep it like that." Rosey and Rylee exchange a look, then nod in agreement. I pull my coat on. "I need my bed," I announce. "Tell Ghost I'll collect my stuff another time."

They watch me in alarm. "You're not going back to the clubhouse?" asks Rosey.

I give an empty laugh. "Where everyone hates me? No. I'm going home to my place. Ghost needs space, and seeing me in his home will make him suffer."

"It's your home too," argues Rylee. "You're his ol' lady until he announces officially to the club."

"We all know that's coming," I say, forcing a sad smile.

I decide to walk home. I need the air because I still feel tired and shaky. I make a mental note to Google whether pregnancy makes hangovers worse.

A group of girls step out of a bar as I pass. They're giggling and that darkness washes over me again. I'm transported back, but this time I'm not cold. I'm being held up against a wall and I can hear people around me. *"She's fine. Can you flag a cab for us?"* I remember Tom's face being close to my own. He was holding me up, and I felt like my body was heavy. My arms hung by my sides, and I couldn't hold my head up. *"She's had too many glasses of champagne,"* he says to someone, laughing. But I only had two. It was two glasses of bubbles. I tried to tell them that, but the words didn't come out.

"Are you okay, love?" a girl asks, gently tapping my shoulder and bringing me back to reality. I nod, pushing my hands into my pockets and continuing along the path. I take a left and make my way to the taxi rank.

Once in the cab, I direct them to the stately home my parents hired out on Saturday. It's busy, meaning there's another party and I'm not dressed for it. I pay the driver and make my way towards the building. A security man steps forward, holding up his hand. "It's a private party, love," he says in a gruff voice.

"I know. I was actually wanting . . ." I trail off and sigh. I don't know what I came here for. Another man steps forward in the same uniform and smiles at me.

"You're the girl from the other night," he tells me. "Your boyfriend had a right job getting you in a cab," he adds, laughing. "Have you recovered?"

"You saw me?" I ask, and he nods. "And I was drunk?"

"Paralytic, love. You couldn't hold your head up, falling all over the place. In the end, he carried you into the cab." I look over in the direction he nods and stare at the line of black cabs parked up, waiting to take guests home. "Eddie'll remember you. He was complaining cos your boyfriend was trying it on in the back of the cab with you. He told him straight, you needed to sleep it off."

"Eddie," I repeat, feeling a glimmer of hope. "Is he around?"

"Yeah." He whistles and waves to one of the cab drivers. A man steps out and makes his way over. "Eddie, you've got a visitor," he says, pointing to me.

Eddie frowns, but as he gets closer, he smiles. "Love, I was so worried about you. Are you okay?" He's got a kind face, and it reminds me of how my grandpa used to look at me.

Tears fill my eyes and I immediately feel silly. "Sorry," I whisper, wiping my eyes.

Eddie looks around in concern and then gently takes my arm and guides me towards his cab. He opens the back door, and I get in. He then gets in the front but twists in his seat to face me. "You look like a girl with the world on your shoulders." He hands me a tissue, and I wipe my eyes.

"I don't remember the hotel," I whisper. "Do you?" I was so confused and panicked when I left Saturday morning, I didn't remember the hotel.

"Yes. The Swan. It's a nasty place on Front Street. Not to be rude, but it's usually frequented by ladies of the night."

"And what time did you drop me off?"

"Around one."

"Was I drunk?"

He nods. "Your boyfriend said you'd had too much champagne. I was gonna refuse the fare. I didn't wanna risk the mess, yah see. Vomit in the cab takes me off the road for the rest of the night. But there was something about you, and I told my Dotty when I got home, I told her I was worried about you."

"Why were you worried?"

"A gut instinct. Things weren't right. I told him to get you to bed and to keep an eye on you, cos you weren't acting right, and you don't seem the type to take drugs."

"So, you thought I'd taken drugs rather than me being drunk?"

"I guess so. You weren't moving right, yah know. You kept falling about in the back and you were silent. Completely silent. What happened?"

I shrug. "That's what I'm trying to find out. That man wasn't my boyfriend," I explain.

Eddie's face morphs into one of regret. "But he told me he was, said you were getting married."

"I met him that night."

"Oh god, I'm so sorry, I didn't realise. Why the hell didn't I realise?" He looks mad at himself. "He was being inappropriate with you, and I still didn't see it. I had to tell him to pack it up or I was gonna make him walk it."

"What was he doing?" I ask in a quiet voce.

He looks uncomfortable. "He had his hand up your dress. I said you were in no fit state. He stopped when I told him. If I'd have known—"

"It's not your fault," I mutter. "I don't suppose you got his address?" I ask, laughing. I could ask my parents, but then they'd ask questions.

"No, love, just the hotel. But maybe they have something?" Tom's wife's words come back to me. They contacted her to pick up the room bill. I nod. "I'll take you there now," he says.

"I don't have cash," I say.

He starts the engine. "I owe you. Don't worry yourself."

Eddie is right, the place is a shit hole and there are women standing around outside clearly waiting to hire the rooms by the hour. "You want me to come in?" he asks.

"Would you mind?" I ask, feeling nervous.

He smiles and turns off the engine. "Let's go find this piece of shit."

The man behind the desk barely looks up from his iPad as football blares from it. "I was here on Saturday night or Sunday morning," I tell him, and he sighs, pausing the game. "The guy I was with, I need his details."

The man laughs. "No chance."

"It's important," I tell him.

"It always is, sweet cheeks, but I have an obligation to my customers."

"Can't you help the lady out?" Eddie asks, sliding something over the desk towards the man. He relents, taking whatever is under Eddie's hand.

"Can you remember a name?" he asks in a bored tone.

"You would remember," says Eddie. "This young lady was being carried by her gentleman friend. She was extremely drunk." I feel myself blush with embarrassment.

The man grins. "That's right, it was the early hours of the morning, I remember." He taps away on the computer and then writes something on a piece of paper. He rips it from the pad and hands it to me. "You didn't get it here."

I take it, stuffing it in my pocket. "Thank you."

Eddie insists on driving me home. "You've been so kind," I say as he pulls to a stop outside my house.

"I wish to God I'd have followed my instincts on Saturday," he says regretfully. "Please call me whenever you need anything at all. My Dotty would love to meet you. She makes the best apple pie." He hands me a business card. "Let me make everything up to you."

"You really don't need to. You've done more than enough."

"Can I at least take a number so I can check on you?"

I smile, nodding. "Dotty is a lucky lady," I tell him, writing my number down for him.

GHOST

It's hard to settle. I stand in the doorway to the bedroom and stare at the empty bed. I hate that she isn't here. Grabbing one of the stupid blankets that Nelly kept on the end of the bed because she said it looked good, I go back downstairs. Star is drinking shots with the other club girls, but she makes a beeline when she spots me getting comfortable on the couch. I've got half a mind to fuck her just to make Nelly feel half the pain I'm currently suffering, but when she tries to grab my belt, I shake my head, turning my back on her and closing my eyes.

"Wow, did you just turn down a club girl?" asks Harriett. I feel her sit on the end of the couch.

"It won't make anything better," I mutter.

"What would make it better?" she asks.

"If I could rewind to Saturday."

"You left her to come to me," she mutters sadly.

I sit up and take her hand. "We argued, and I walked out. Please don't blame yourself or I'll feel even worse."

"Do you think you can forgive her?"

I shake my head. "No. Why would she do that to me, to us? I gave her everything she needed in and out the bedroom. It makes no sense."

"Talk to her. Listen to her side."

"I can't right now, H. I'm so fucking mad, and then she cries and my heart hurts all over again. I can't bear to see her upset, even when it's her fault. And now, she's carrying my kid and I can't just fucking walk away and turn this damn pain in my chest off."

"Give it time and maybe you'll forgive her."

"I want what my parents have," I say. "A solid marriage. How can I ever trust her after this?"

"People make mistakes, Ghost. It's still very early in your relationship. Why are you sleeping on the couch?"

"Cos I can't fucking bear to be in that room when she isn't there," I mutter bitterly.

Harriett smiles. "Heartbreak is the worst thing ever, but forgiveness feels so much better. You know what it feels like not to have her and you hate it. Go and see her, Ghost. Make up. Be together. Life is too short to be miserable." She kisses me on the cheek. "I'm going to bed. Please think about it."

At some point in the middle of the night, when I give up on sleep, I have a kind of out of body experience. One that takes me to Nelly. And as I stand at the end of her bed watching her sleep, I wonder how the fuck I'm gonna let her go. How will I see her with my kid in her arms and not feel something? She's gonna be the hardest thing I've ever had get over.

She stirs and a part of me thinks about leaving, but I'm rooted to the spot. She's unsettled, occasionally flinching in her sleep or letting a small moan escape her lips, and a bitter part of me wonders if she's dreaming about him, whoever *he* is. I lower onto the end of the bed, running a finger over her bare ankle, wondering if it will be the last time I get to touch her skin. She takes me by surprise when she bolts upright and begins screaming. I clamp my hand over her mouth to muffle the sound. It's an instant reaction, and in the moonlight, I see the terror in her eyes.

"It's me," I whisper. "It's just me. Calm the fuck down." She stops the noise, but when I remove my hand, it's replaced with large, heavy sobs. "Sorry, I didn't mean to scare you." I watch her cry, itching to pull her into my arms and fighting with myself not to.

She eventually gets herself together. "You scared me. How did you get in?"

"Were you going to tell me?" It's a question that's played on my mind since I found out.

"You can't just turn up here and creep around."

"Were you planning on dumping me for him?"

"No."

"Why did you do it?"

"I was drunk," she whispers feebly. "I don't remember."

"People get drunk all the time and don't end up cheating, Nelly. If you weren't happy with me, you should have told me."

"I am happy, Ghost. I didn't mean for it to happen. I—"

"There's no excuse," I say. "Why am I even here?" I scrub my hands over my tired face. "What does it really matter why you did it? The fact is, you did and now we're done. But you're carrying my kid, and I have to decide how I parent a kid with you when I fucking hate you." Pain fills her expression. "Maybe I won't hate you so much when it's time to have this kid. Maybe I'm just so fucking angry that it's all I can feel right now. You blindsided me, Nelly. I didn't see it coming."

"I tried to warn you," she tells me, getting up from the bed and grabbing a shirt. She pulls it on and turns to look at me. Her eyes are swollen, and she looks so lost and broken. "I always mess up. I always disappoint. I was never good enough for you, Ghost, and I tried to tell you, and you promised you'd stick around."

"You want me to stick around while you fuck other men?" I yell in disbelief.

"No . . . I . . . it wasn't my . . . I was . . ." She sighs, shaking her head. "Just leave."

She doesn't get to tell me what to do, and I'm not ready to leave. My mobile buzzes and I stare at Mav's name. "What?" I snap, answering it.

"I take it you're with her?" he asks.

"She's fine, if that's what you're worried about."

"Of course, I'm not, brother. I know you'd never hurt her. Prescott has the money. He's had a big win on the tables, so Arthur just called me. Shall we meet at his office?"

"On my way."

CHAPTER SEVENTEEN

GHOST

Prescott is stepping out his office with his keys in his hand, ready to lock up. I put my hand firmly on his shoulder and guide him back inside. "I'm so happy you got the money together," I tell him. "We thought we'd save you a telephone call and show up now."

"You guys are up and about early, but like I've already told you, I don't have it."

"Now you're telling me lies?" I ask. I pull my fist back and hit him in the stomach. He bends, coughing violently. "I hate lies."

Mav picks up a bag from the doorway and places it on the desk. Inside are bundles of cash and some passports. He opens a couple of them up and laughs. "Were you thinking of going on holiday, Isaac Johnson? How many identities have you got in here?"

"The money isn't mine," he splutters.

"You're right. It belongs to the Fletchers, and that's exactly where it's going when I leave here," I tell him.

"But the men I owe it to will come looking for it."

"Not my problem."

"They'll kill me."

"Again, not my problem."

Mav zips up the bag. "We'll be back next week to collect Mr. Taylor's money. And just so you know, if you're still alive, which I doubt you will be knowing some of the men you owe to, but if you are, Mr. Taylor requested we remove a finger for every thousand you're late paying."

"But you're taking everything I have," he cries.

I slap him on the back hard. "Maybe it's time you changed your career. You're not very good at being a conman."

I get on my bike and ride. It's the longest ride out I've had in a while, and when I finally pull to a stop outside Nelly's parents' house, my body aches, but fuck do I feel good. There's something about that open road that cleanses my mind. Maybe I need to hit it for a few months and get away from the shit.

The house is just as Nelly described it with a front garden full of flowers. I tap on the door, and Adam answers, his smile fading. "Eric, is Nelly okay?"

I nod, smiling. "Yeah, I'm not here about Nelly. In fact, she doesn't know I'm here."

He frowns and opens the door wider. "You'd better come in."

I follow him down the hall, where the walls are full of photographs of Nelly growing up. I pause at a recent one of me and her together. We're not aware of the photographer, but it was taken on that night... the night she cheated on me. We're looking at each other with such love, you'd never see what was about to come. "We'd hired a photographer," explains Adam when he notices I've stopped. "We got the pictures back recently, and Charlotte insisted we put it up."

Once in the kitchen, he calls Charlotte in from the back garden. We wait in silence for her to join us. She pulls off her gardening gloves and smiles wide, wrapping her arms around me in a hug. "What a lovely surprise. Where's Nelly?"

"She doesn't know he's here," Adam explains.

"I wanted to come in person to tell you this myself," I begin, and they both take a seat at the table.

"Oh no, have you split up?" gasps Charlotte.

I decide not to answer rather than lie. "It's about your villa." Relief passes over both their faces, and I hate I'm about to ruin their dream. "It's not real. Tom Prescott is scamming you."

Adam laughs. "You had me there."

"It's not a joke."

His smile fades. "Of course, it's real. We paid the deposit. We saw the pictures."

I reach into my bag and pull out the envelope of pictures I have, some with the plans and fake builds and some with the actual plot of land. "I had someone check it out. There's nothing there. In fact, nothing can be built on this land because it's been deemed unfit for builds."

"You're wrong. Hugo's been to see it. He was the one who told us about it." That confirms my suspicions.

"I wish I was wrong, but I promise I'm not."

"We paid a deposit," Charlotte says, looking panicked.

I dump the bag of money on the table. "It's all there, with a little extra for the inconvenience."

Adam peers into the bag. "Jesus, where did you get that?"

"Tom Prescott was more than understanding when I explained I wasn't very happy. He got the cash together pretty quickly."

"That was very lucky," says Adam with a slight smirk.

"Oh, Eric," gasps Charlotte, also staring at the cash. "Thank you so much. I don't know how we'll ever repay you. We were about to invest everything into that move."

"I'm just happy we got your money back," I tell her.

"Nelly must think we're so stupid," she mutters.

"She doesn't know. I told her I was suspicious, but she left me to deal with it."

They look relieved. "We try to keep things like this from her so she doesn't worry. She's been through so much in her life. Maybe we shelter her a little too much."

"She told me about Lucy," I say, hoping I don't upset them, but Charlotte looks relieved.

"She did? That's great. We get so worried because she never speaks about her. The therapist told us it was normal, but we thought once she got older, she'd mention her at least. I used to think she'd forgotten, because of the trauma, yah know?"

"She said when she'd speak about it, you'd get upset, so she stopped."

They exchange a sad look. "It was hard not to cry. We loved her so much, we all did, and it was hard losing her the way we did. There was so much guilt. If I hadn't had been asleep, it wouldn't have happened." Adam rubs her arm in a comforting move.

"She told me you were ill," I say.

"I was tired, not ill. I took a day nap."

I arch my brows in surprise. All this time and they were both blaming themselves, letting guilt eat away at them. "You should really talk about it. Nelly feels like it was all on her."

"Let's have some coffee," suggests Adam. "All this excitement in one day is too much for my heart."

NELLY

I wring my hands together, pacing back and forth, occasionally looking at the office door. I have to do this. I need answers. The flashbacks are becoming unbearable, and I don't know if it's guilt that keeps me awake at night or because, deep down, I think something bad did happen to me. All the evidence certainly points that way.

I've spent the last few days tracking Tom Prescott down, following him as he plays happy family with his wife and splits his time between home, a very expensive house in Westminster, and this rundown office on the other side of the river. It doesn't quite add up.

I wait for his assistant to leave for the day before taking a deep breath and forcing myself to approach the door, all the while wanting to run away. I push it open and step inside. The reception area is empty, but the office door to the left is open and that's where I find him. He looks up and smirks when he sees me, throwing his pen down and leaning back in his chair. He doesn't look surprised.

"You come back for seconds?" he asks. He's got two black eyes and a busted lip. It's obvious he's upset somebody recently. "I gotta tell yah, I don't usually fuck the same person twice, but I've had a really fucking bad week, so I'm willing to let you help me forget."

"Forget," I repeat. "Maybe there's a drug you can take for that."

His expression gives nothing away. "Why are you here, Nelly? You look like shit. When did you last sleep?"

"Thanks to you, a good while ago."

"Are you one of those women who hates rejection?" he asks, wincing.

"Why didn't I remember it?" I ask. "Why is it only coming back to me in pieces?" I underestimated how much his voice would trigger me and I'm shaking uncontrollably.

"Have you taken something?" he asks, standing up.

"I just want to know what happened?" I snap.

"We had sex."

"In the hotel?" I ask.

He grins like he's humouring me, like I've lost my mind. "Yes."

"So, why can I remember being outside?"

"I don't know, Nelly. Did you have sex before me?"

I frown, that thought scaring the hell out of me. I'm working through the questions in my mind, and suddenly, he's by the door. I move away from him, my legs hitting against the desk. "Relax, I'm just getting ready to make my own escape, because you turning up here looking all dishevelled and, frankly, fucking crazy, has me on edge."

"I have you on edge?" I ask, half laughing and half crying. "You did something to me. I know you did."

"We had sex, Nelly. People have sex. Were you a virgin or something, because Hugo told me you were up for it."

My blood runs cold. "What?"

"He said you love it, sex. Like you were a nymphomaniac or something."

I shake my head, tears dripping from my chin. "You drugged me."

"You were drunk."

"No, I wasn't," I yell. "You drugged me, and you had sex with me, but I didn't want to. I didn't want to have sex with you." Tom's expression changes. He's mad, and he slams the office door and locks it. Fear grips me and I remember that look in his eyes. He prowls towards me, and I back away around the desk. "You raped me," I say in a low voice. "You drugged me and raped me." I thought that by saying the words out loud, they would set me free. That this ache in my stomach would leave, but it's still here.

"Prove it," he hisses.

"I can't. You know I can't. So, just tell me so I can stop the doubt in my mind." My tone is pleading, and he grins. He doesn't give a shit that I'm going out of my mind.

"You wanted it."

"I didn't. You're lying."

He keeps moving closer, and I keep moving away. "Why are you torturing yourself with these questions, Nelly? You enjoyed it. I left you satisfied."

"I didn't want it," I say through gritted teeth.

"Whores always want it. Hugo told me about your affair, the things you'd do for him. Even though you knew he was married." He moves fast, too fast, and catches my arm, dragging me to him. "And I wanted some of that tight little cunt," he adds, laughing when I try to break free. "But maybe you're right." He pushes me back onto the desk. "Maybe I shouldn't have drugged you. I like a fight." Terror stops me feeling relief at his confession. I've put myself in danger again, and I have no idea how the fuck to get away. Taking a breath to calm myself, I can't think straight, but I remember that whenever Rob would pin me like this, I'd always manage to talk him down.

"What about your wife?"

He holds my hands above my head. "What about her?"

"She paid me a visit. She knows all about me." It's new information to him and he frowns. "I told her I couldn't get enough of you. She was so mad, she talked about speaking to her father." It's a wild guess, but it hits a nerve, and he glares down at me.

"Why did you tell her that?" he growls.

"Because that's what you said."

"You stupid bitch," he snaps, releasing my hands to unfasten his jeans. I struggle, trying desperately to kick him off me, but it doesn't work. Flipping me over so I'm face down, he pulls my leggings over my arse. There's an ink pen within reach, the sort you'd use as a teenager, that you had to put a cartridge inside to make it work. He's distracted, trying to pull my knickers down while I flail my legs around, so he doesn't see me grab the pen. "Stay fucking still or

I'll suffocate you," he yells, yanking my head back by my hair.

"I'm pregnant," I yell. "Please, I can't lay like this." His weight briefly comes away and he turns me back over. I hold the pen to my side. "You were so much more compliant before," he whispers, looking amused. "I fucked you till my dick was sore, and you didn't even flinch. But having you fight me feels so much more exciting." I lie still, staring up at him blankly. "You think I won't do it if you lie like a good girl?" he asks, groping my breast through my shirt. He suddenly slaps me across the face, and I cry out. "That's better. Now, fucking fight." His hand squeezes around my neck, cutting off my air, while the other continues to pull at my clothes.

I grip the pen tightly, bringing my arm higher. He looks up, confused, but before he can work out my next move, I slam the pen into his neck. I feel it slide in without any resistance. His eyes widen and he tries to speak, but nothing comes out. I don't flinch when blood runs over my fingers and onto my face and chest, dripping like a leaky tap. He feels me begin to withdraw the pen and panics, grabbing it and trying to hold my hand in place. But it's too wet for him to get a good grip, and I tug, watching as blood pours from the wound I just inflicted. He gasps, placing his hand over the hole. His erection is no longer pushing against me, and as I slam the pen into his eye, I scream as a rage burns inside of me.

"You piece of fucking shit!" I yell. "You raped me! You fucking raped me!" Minutes pass before I realise he isn't making a sound. I shove him from me, and he falls onto the desk and then onto the floor with a loud thud. I sit up and stare down at his still body, nudging him hard with my foot, but he doesn't groan.

"Oh, fuck," I whisper, seeing the blood on my hands and realising what I've just done. With a shaky hand, I pull out my mobile and dial Rosey's number.

"Hey, lady, how are you?" she asks cheerfully.

"I need your help. I did something."

"Where are you?" I reel off the address. "On my way," she says, disconnecting.

I wait by the door, occasionally peeking through the blind. When I see Rosey's car come to a stop with Rylee in the passenger seat, I sag with relief. I open the door and let them inside. They both stare at the blood on my hands, face, and shirt.

"What the fuck happened?" asks Rosey.

I lead them into the office where Tom is face down on the floor. "Holy shit," gasps Rylee.

"Who is that?" asks Rosey.

"Tom Prescott," I mutter.

"The guy?" screeches Rylee, and I nod. "Shit."

"He admitted it," I say in a quiet voice. My hands are still shaking badly, so I fold my arms.

"That's great, Nelly, but what do we do with a confession from a dead man?" asks Rosey, swooping down to check his pulse. She shakes her head to confirm he's dead.

"Oh, fuck," I cry, covering my mouth with my shaking blood-stained hands. "I killed him."

"It's okay," soothes Rylee, rubbing my arms. "It'll be fine."

CHAPTER EIGHTEEN

GHOST

I get back into London pretty late after spending a few hours with Nelly's parents. I'm not sure why I agreed to stay for lunch, but it seemed the right thing to do. Stopping outside the club, I find Rylee outside, pacing. I frown. "You okay?" I ask, removing my helmet.

"We tried to call you," she says, and I'm immediately worried. "Nelly got herself into a spot of bother."

I get off the bike. "Is she okay?"

"Not really. She's inside."

I barge into the club and freeze when I see Nelly 'ered in blood. She's pale and shaking. "What the happened?" I snap. "Are you hurt?"

shakes her head. "Ghost, get in here," yells Mav he room where we hold church.

Inside, all the brothers are gathered. "We've been calling," snaps Grim.

"What happened?"

"She killed Tom Prescott," says Mav.

I fall into my seat, too shocked to react for a minute. "What?"

"He tried to attack her," he adds.

"Why was she even there? I only told her parents today, and I know they didn't tell her because they made me promise to keep it from her too."

"It was nothing to do with them. I'll fill you in right after we work out our next move. I got the clean-up to take care of the body, and Arthur is on his way here. We need to prepare for the fact that he's gonna be missed. We need to come up with something."

"And not to shit on the pile, but you told her parents he was a conman and now he's dead. That doesn't look suspicious at all," says Grim sarcastically.

"Fuckkk," I groan, burying my head in my hands.

"I'm gonna speak to Ghost in private," says Mav, and he and Grim stand. "The rest of you stay here and think of a plan. We'll be back."

I follow them into Mav's office. My adrenaline is already pumping, and by the look on their faces, it ain't about to slow down anytime soon. "Just tell me," I say firmly, needing this to be over.

"Sit down," Grim tells me.

"Now I'm getting worried." I lower into the chair, and they do the same.

"Nelly didn't cheat on you," Mav begins.

"Pres, she looked me in the eye and told me she did."

He shakes his head. "She was attacked. Drugged and attacked."

I take a second to process what he's telling me. "But . . . no . . . she said—"

"She couldn't remember, and then she went into denial. Tom Prescott drugged and raped her." I suck in a painful breath at his words. "He made her think she'd willingly had sex with him, that she'd just been too drunk to recall events, but as the days went on, her memory started to come back."

I hunch over, trying to catch my breath. Suddenly, the air feels tight in here and sickness swirls in the pit of my stomach. I picture Nelly's face, her tear-stained, swollen face, and a choked sob leaves me. Grim pats my back, "It's a lot to take in, brother," he says quietly. "If he was still alive, I'd fucking kill him all over again."

"I should have realised when she was acting so weird. I just thought she felt guilty."

"It's not your fault. She told you she cheated, so how were you supposed to know?" asks Mav. "Brother, she needs you now more than ever. She's a fucking mess. She needs a shower and to get them clothes off. They've gotta get burned ASAP. We don't know if anyone saw her going in or out. Fuck, it's a mess."

I nod, standing. "Are you sure you're gonna be okay?" asks Grim, looking worried. I nod again, leaving the office.

I step out and see Nelly. She's by the bar, staring into space while the other women surround her, gently speaking to her like she's a small lost child. I take a deep breath and march over. "We gotta get you out those clothes, Nelly," I say sharply, getting my MC head on. It works, bringing her from her daydream to look at me. I need to feel her against me. My entire being is calling to hers, and so I scoop her into my arms and head for the stairs. She rests her head on my shoulder, and I'm relieved she hasn't push me away.

Once we're in my room, I lower her to stand and then I go into the bathroom and turn on the shower. "Are you hurt anywhere?" I ask, entering the bedroom where she's still in the exact same spot I left her. "Nelly, are you hurt?" She shakes her head. "Can you undress?" After a few seconds of silence, I take her by the hand and gently lead her to the bathroom. Taking her hands, I place them on my chest. "I'm gonna go real slow, and you can tell me to stop at any time. We'll do this at your pace. Okay?" She nods. "Words, baby."

"Okay," she whispers.

I remove her clothing piece by piece, noting there's a rip in her leggings as I discard them. There's bruising to her neck, chest, thigh, and face. I remove my boots and kutte, then place her hands back to my chest. I step backwards into the shower, fully clothed, and position her under the water. She closes her eyes, tipping her head back as I grab the soap and lather a sponge. "Do you want me to wash, or you?"

"You," she murmurs.

I wash away the dried blood, taking extra care to scrub under her nails with a brush. I shampoo her hair, massaging her head, just the way she likes. All the while, a million questions race around my head.

Once she's clean, I turn the shower off and wrap her in a large fluffy towel. She waits while I strip off my wet clothes and throw them in a pile with hers and also wrap myself in a towel. "What will happen now?" she asks.

In the bedroom, she sits on the edge of the bed while I search for something for her to wear. I'd already removed her clothes from the wardrobe, so I take out one of my shirts. "The club will sort it."

"I killed him," she murmurs. "I killed him."

"He deserved it," I say bitterly.

"I'm going to go to prison. Oh god, I can't go to prison. What about my parents, what about the baby?"

I crouch in front of her, making eye contact. "You're not going to prison, Nelly. I know it feels huge right now, but every day that passes, it will get easier."

"I have to confess," she says, trying to stand, but I keep her seated. "But if I tell the police what he did, how he . . ." She stops.

"How he?" I push. She needs to say the words out loud.

"He . . . how he . . . he . . ."

"It's okay. You can say the words. They're just words."

She shakes her head. "They'll change everything."

"Nelly, things won't be the same even if you don't say the words."

She wipes her wet cheeks with her hands. "But then it's real," she whispers with a sad smile, and I nod. "I'm not ready for it to be real."

I take her hand and push it through the arm of my shirt, doing the same with the other side, then removing the towel and fastening it. I help her into a pair of my boxer briefs, which are too big, but she's not going anywhere. I pull the sheets back from the bed, and she climbs inside. There're sleeping pills in the bathroom, which I give her, and she swallows gratefully. "Sleep, baby."

"Will you be here when I wake up?" she asks. I nod, gently stroking her hair and waiting for her to drift off.

NELLY

I open my eyes and, true to his word, Ghost is sitting beside me on the bed. He's watching me, and

I know he must have questions. "I spent the day with your parents," he tells me.

"Why?" I ask, confused.

"I went to see them about the villa in France. It was a con. Tom Prescott is . . . was a conman."

"You still did that, even though we'd split up?"

"Is your name still on my chest?" he asks, and I nod. "Then you're still my ol' lady."

"You must have questions," I say, dreading his response. I'm not sure I'm ready to talk about any of it, but he deserves to know.

"So many questions," he mutters, shaking his head. "But I'm gonna wait because you're not ready."

"I really thought I'd cheated," I add in a low voice.

"I wish you'd told me everything that happened that night, the bits you remembered."

"Rosey thought it was odd. She tried to get me to tell you and said you'd think the same as her, but I was terrified. I didn't want to give you false hope and let you down."

He tucks my hair behind my ear. "Baby, stop trying to save everyone. You're just hurting yourself by holding all this guilt you take on. I spoke about Lucy, to your parents." I gasp. "They want to talk about her. They didn't because your mum holds guilt too. She blames herself, you blame yourself, and no one talked."

"Why does she blame herself?"

"I'm not doing the talking for you, baby. You gotta speak to her yourself and work shit out. But what

I will say is, no one was to blame but the driver of the car. You all lost Lucy because of him, and I don't think he spends his nights blaming himself because he never got the balls to step up and admit what he'd done."

I bury my face in my hands. "I know you're right, but I just can't shake it. And now, my poor parents can't retire to their dream villa. How much did they lose?"

Ghost grins. "Baby, you think I didn't get back every penny they were owed?"

Relief floods me. "You did?"

"And a little extra for their troubles. I told you to trust me on it, that I'd never intentionally let you down." He takes a deep breath. "Which brings me to that night. I'm so fucking sorry I left you, Nelly. If I hadn't gone early—"

"Hindsight is a great power," I say, smiling sadly. "You didn't know, Ghost. I stupidly accepted a drink from him because I wanted to get to the bottom of the villa."

"If I could kill him all over again, I would."

Flashes of Tom's wide, panicked eyes fill my head and sickness bubbles in my throat. "What if the police come?"

I take her hands in mine. "They will, Nelly. They're gonna come because there's connections, but we'll talk you through it. You just gotta be a good liar with a poker face."

"Neither of which I have," I wail. "I'll have our baby in prison."

He smiles, taking my face in his hands. "You'll never go to prison. I'll confess before that happens."

"It's not fair," I mutter. "He hurt me, and he was going to do it again. I just wanted him to stop."

"It's all gonna be okay. I promise."

CHAPTER NINETEEN

GHOST

Shoving Nelly's clothes into the burner, I stare as the blue and orange flames swallow the garments. "She okay?" Scar asks as he joins me.

"Not really. I gave her more pills to sleep. I don't know what else to do."

"Just g-give her t-time. Did you get Doc to ch-check her?"

I nod. Doc examined her and did another scan on the baby. He confirmed all is well, and although there could be side effects for the baby from the drug Prescott gave her, only time will tell. "He gave her a mild sleeping pill and said other than rest, there's not much we can do. He said her memories might fully come back or they might just stay as flashbacks. I hope they don't come back cos she doesn't want that shit in her head."

"A-are you okay?"

I shrug. "Mad I can't fucking pull him apart limb by limb. Pissed he's free of what he did. He needed to suffer, and instead, he died with a fucking hard-on for my ol' lady. The old me would have killed his entire family for what he did to her. I'm doing everything I can to control that side of me."

"You're h-holding it t-together well, bro."

Mav comes over and peers into the fire pit. "Clothes?" he asks, and I nod. "I just got the heads-up that he's been reported as missing."

"It took two days for them to report him, so what does that say about him? No one could give a shit. Let's bury this and move on," I snap.

"We just gotta get Nelly up and about in case the cops make an appearance."

I wake Nelly with a gentle kiss to her forehead. She eventually forces her eyes open, and I smile at her sleepy face. I love her so damn much, but my heart breaks for her. "Hey, we gotta start getting you up and moving."

"I don't want to," she murmurs, closing her eyes again.

"It's not a choice, baby. If the cops come around, it'll look suspicious that you're in bed all day. We gotta practise your story."

She sighs heavily, throwing the covers back. "Why can't we just tell them he was a bastard who hurt women? They can see from my bruises there was a fight."

"We've been over this. It's your word against his and there's no proof. His wife already knows you had sex with him. They're gonna come looking here."

I wait while she showers and gets dressed, then we go down to the office where Pres and Grim are waiting. They offer her a sympathetic smile as she takes a seat beside me. "How are you?" asks Grim.

"Tired," she mutters.

"Prescott was reported missing this morning. His wife filed the report and said she hadn't seen him for a couple of days. She said she thought he was busy with work, but when she contacted the office, his assistant told her she hadn't seen him since Monday evening. There's been no mention of him having a visitor, so she didn't see you."

"I waited till she'd gone," says Nelly.

"We got all the CCTV cameras and wiped them. Grim checked for cameras on nearby buildings and couldn't find any. So, without any real evidence, they won't have any reason to come for you. But they will turn up and ask, Nelly. His wife knew you'd had sex, and she also knows where to find you. Plus, there's a connection with your parents, so it all looks suspicious."

"I'm a terrible liar," she admits.

"You'll be amazed how good you can be when it's a choice of freedom or prison," says Grim.

"So, here's what you say," instructs Mav.

NELLY

Two more days have passed, and we haven't had any visits from the police. Mav's informant said there is an investigation and there was an appeal on social media about Tom Prescott being treated as a missing person. I'm tense and stressed, and the thought of lying makes me sick to my stomach, but Mav is right, it's a necessary lie to keep me out of prison. And I can't go to prison. Honestly, I think the nightmares of his face will haunt me for the rest of my life, coupled with flashbacks of him hurting me, and I'm practically in my own prison of hell.

"Nelly," says Tiny, the prospect, "you have a visitor."

Ghost appears from the office like an alert animal. "All visitors have to go through me," he growls.

"Sorry, brother, I forgot," mutters Tiny.

"It's fine," I say. "Who is it?"

"Some old guy, Eddie."

I smile. "Let him through."

"Who is he?" asks Ghost, taking my hand. Since everything came out, he's been amazing, sticking to my side at every waking moment, but we haven't discussed our relationship, or if we even still have one.

"He knows what happened to me," I tell Ghost. "He was the cab driver who helped me piece some things together." I'd already told Ghost about the night I tracked Tom Prescott down and my visit to the hotel.

Eddie steps into the clubhouse, and I rush to him. He embraces me and it makes me feel warm inside. He takes me by the shoulders and holds me at arm's length. "I have to be quick. The police have been to see me and—"

"Miss Fletcher?" comes a voice from behind Eddie.

Tiny stands with two female police officers. "Sorry, Pres," he says to Mav. "They came in when I was showing the old guy through. I tried to stop them."

Mav steps forward. "It's fine, Tiny. London's finest are always welcome at The Perished Riders compound. What can we help you with?"

"We're here to speak with Nelly Fletcher."

Eddie places a protective arm around my shoulders and gives a gentle squeeze. "That's me," I say, but my voice sounds detached from my body.

"Is there somewhere private we can go?"

"I already told you, she was with me on Monday night," snaps Eddie. "We were having tea with my good wife, Dotty. You can call and ask her." I want to hug him tightly for giving me an alibi with no questions asked.

One of the officers smiles tightly. "It's not really about that. We need to speak to Nelly alone."

"That ain't happening," snaps Ghost, taking my hand. "She's my ol' lady and you know how that shit works. You wanna talk to her, you gotta go through me."

"Your gang rules don't apply to the Metropolitan Police," she states coldly. "I'll speak with you present, but only if Miss Fletcher approves it."

I nod. "And the Pres," I add.

We all go into Mav's office. I'm shaking so bad, I have to hold onto Ghost. "We're investigating the disappearance of a local businessman, Elliot Smith, but you might know him as Tom Prescott," she begins. She holds up a photograph of Prescott, and I run my eyes over it, keeping my face straight like Mav taught me. "Do you know him?"

I nod. "Yes, he was doing business with my parents."

"Not business. He was conning her parents," snaps Ghost.

"We know about that," she says, "but that's not why we're here."

"So, get to the point," he says impatiently.

"While investigating, we came across a mobile phone. It belongs to Hugo Woods. Do you know him?" she asks. I nod again, this time staying quiet. Mav told me the police sometimes wait for you to over-talk and that's how they know you're hiding something. "The phone belongs to him. Anyway, while retrieving messages between Hugo and the missing person, we came across a deleted file. The file contained videos." She swallows hard, glancing nervously at the other officer. "You were in those videos, Miss. Fletcher."

I frown. I didn't practise this with the guys. This wasn't what we were expecting. "What sort of videos?" asks Ghost.

"We don't think Nelly was . . . aware she was being filmed."

My blood runs cold and I can hear the loud pulse of my heart in my ears. "Hugo's phone?" I repeat.

She nods sadly. "Nelly, we think you may have been drugged right before those videos were filmed. Do you have any idea what I'm talking about?" she asks gently. I nod, my eyes filling with ears. "So, you know what happened to you?"

"I have flashbacks, not memories. But I didn't want to believe it," I murmur.

"This will be really hard for you, but we need to show you a snippet of the video. We need to identify who was there."

"What do you mean?" I ask. "It was him, Prescott. He was there. He tol—"

"Nelly," Mav warns firmly, and I press my lips together. "Officer, this is all a huge shock. Nelly thought something bad had happened, but she wasn't completely sure, and you've just confirmed it. Ghost can identify those in the video. He met both men."

GHOST

The officer nods, and Mav turns to Nelly. "Go to Rylee and stay with her until I come find you." She rushes from the office without a word.

"Just out of interest," asks the officer, "where did she get those bruises?"

I exchange a look with Mav. "She caught me with a club girl, and they got into a fight." I'd rather pretend I cheated on my own ol' lady than them suspect she was involved in anything to do with Prescott's disappearance. "Star will confirm."

The officer produces a mobile phone in a plastic bag and holds it out for me to look at. "Are you sure you're ready for this?" she asks, and I nod. She presses play, and I hear Hugo's voice straightaway. His annoying laugh and words of hate fill my ears as he films Nelly on the ground. She's still, her eyes half closed, while Prescott grips her neck and rips open her top.

"They were both there," I mutter.

"Can you confirm the men in the video?" asks the officer.

"The man on top of my ol' lady, about to rape her, is Tom Prescott. The man filming is Hugo Woods."

"And how certain are you?"

"A thousand percent. I know his voice anywhere. There's no doubt in my mind."

She presses stop, and I sigh in relief. I can't bring myself to look at her as she tucks the phone away. "At some point, Nelly will need to give a statement."

"What if she doesn't want to?" I ask.

"Why wouldn't she?"

"She's scared and confused," I snap. "She's about to find out that a man she used to be intimate with had filmed her attack and laughed through it."

"Off the record," says the other cop, who had been quiet up until now, "we think Woods might have had something to do with Prescott's disappearance. We know that Prescott blackmailed him with the recording and threatened to tell his wife, his business partners, and Nelly herself, if he didn't give him cash."

"But that's strictly off the record," snaps the first officer, who gives her colleague a pointed stare. "We don't know what happened yet, but if Nelly isn't comfortable coming forward, we can use the video evidence anyway. We just need a statement from either one of you to confirm everyone in that video."

"Will it implicate her in your investigation?" asks Mav.

The officer shakes her head. "No, Nelly has an alibi, right? Eddie, the cab driver?"

I nod. "Yes, she was having tea with him and his wife. He's been a great support to Nelly. In fact, he was the taxi driver that night of the attack. He can confirm Prescott was with her and that she didn't appear to be of a consenting state."

NELLY

I hand Eddie a cup of tea. "Why did you lie for me?" I ask, just as Ghost comes into the kitchen. I introduce the pair properly, and we all sit down.

"It wasn't a lie. You came for tea," he tells me, smiling. "You'll need to come again if your memory is hazy."

I smile. "That would be nice."

"What happened to you was disgusting, and whatever might have happened to that sleezebag was justice. The kind that will take him directly to hell. You'll never get that if you drag it through the courts. I, for one, am happy he's missing. I hope he never returns."

Ghost nods in agreement. "Me too. I owe you for helping my ol' lady."

"I wish I'd have stepped in that night. I'll live with that guilt forever."

"I wish I'd never have left her, and I'll live with that guilt forever," says Ghost.

"And I wish I'd never met him or accepted that first drink, I'll regret that forever," I say. "But someone told me I had to stop taking on the guilt of another's actions. And he was right. I should be able to accept a drink and not expect be drugged or . . . raped." The second the words leave my lips, I feel lighter. "I should be able to ride my bike to the shop and not have an irresponsible prick run into my sister and kill her. I'm done feeling guilt for things out of my control. I don't blame either of you for that night. I blame Tom Prescott. So, may his body rest in the depths of hell and may the devil torture him for eternity and may he rot in his own piss and shit."

Ghost grins. "Cheers to that, baby."

CHAPTER TWENTY

Three months later...
NELLY

Ghost lays between my legs with his hands either side of my small bump. "I can't, not with the little man inside there," he tells me.

I bite my lower lip to stop from smiling. I'm supposed to be mad. "Sex won't hurt him. I asked Doc."

"Who took the piss out of me, so thanks for that," he says, his voice dripping with sarcasm.

"My hormones are on another level," I complain. "If you don't help me out, I'm going to sort it myself."

Ghost smirks, his eyes darkening. "Tell me some more about that." I shake my head in exasperation. Getting Ghost to touch me since my bump appeared is like asking the Pope for a one-night stand—it ain't gonna happen.

Since my attack, and after a few sessions of therapy, we've had sex a handful of times. It's enough to make me forget Prescott's hands on me but not enough to stop this new horny feeling I have constantly. "I'll meet you halfway," he offers, shifting my panties to one side and running his tongue along my opening. I hiss, fisting the bed sheets.

"I'm not bargaining. Just fuck me already," I hiss.

Ghost laughs. "Take it or leave it," he adds, rubbing my swollen clit.

A knock at the door interrupts us. I growl in frustration when Ghost jumps from the bed, adjusting his obvious erection in his jeans. He swings it open, and Dice smiles. "Hey, the Pres sent me to get you. People are arriving."

"They won't notice if we're not there," I snap angrily, and Ghost laughs harder.

"Ignore her, she's in a mood."

"Dice, what are your thoughts on sex and pregnant women?" I ask innocently.

Ghost slams the door in his face before he can answer and dives over me, taking his weight on his arms and knees. "Woman, you're gonna drive me crazy," he growls, nipping the delicate skin on my neck. "We have a party to get to."

"You're choosing a party over the needs of your ol' lady?"

He buries his head in my neck and groans. The door crashes open and Scar stands there. "Downstairs, n-now," he orders.

"You sent an SOS call to your brother," I accuse. I know Scar and Ghost have a deal where they can call each other for help anytime.

"Y-your parents have arrived," he says. "Eddie and his w-wife are here. P-put my brother d-down for two minutes."

Ghost helps me from the bed and makes sure my dress is in place. He high fives his brother before leading me downstairs where our guests await the gender reveal. It was Meli's idea. She wanted something to cheer everyone up, and I suspect to take my mind off everything. Even Ghost didn't argue when she announced she was planning it.

My parents embrace me. They only recently learned of my attack. It had to come out in the open because I was called to give evidence alongside them at the trial last month. Hugo was arrested for the murder of Elliot Smith, or Tom, whatever he called himself. He had so many aliases, I've lost track. I felt bad at first, knowing Hugo was taking the blame for something I did, but when I was played the videos of my attack, I realised he was as much a part of my rape as Tom was. He watched, jerked himself off, whispered words of hate in my ear, and then encouraged Tom to take me back to that hotel and make up a lie so I'd believe I willingly had sex with him. And it was all so he could use it to blackmail him out of his wife's money.

Eddie and Dotty are also waiting to greet us. They've become like adopted grandparents around the club. Dotty even comes to the women's centre one day a week to help out. She makes the best tea and apple pie, and all the women adore her. "I have a bet with Eddie," she tells me in a conspiring whisper. "If it's a girl, he owes me lunch at Ridleys."

"Which is a week's worth of cab fares," says Eddie, shaking his head.

"Well, I can tell you, it's a boy," says Ghost, who's believed that since I said I was pregnant.

"Let's hope so," says Eddie, rubbing his hands together. "I can have a whole weekend at the fishing lake if it is."

Meli stands on one of the garden tables and claps her hands to get attention. When she's satisfied all eyes are on her, she smiles. "I've filmed every single guest," she tells us, "and the consensus is, it's a girl. But only I know the truth, so, Maverick, start your engine." She throws the Pres his bike keys, and he rolls his eyes at the build-up. I laugh as he shakes his head and throws a leg over his bike. He puts the key in the ignition as Ghost pulls me tight into his side. I know he'll be thrilled whatever the sex, but his reasoning for a boy is to protect all our future daughters, which is kind of sweet.

The engine starts and Mav revs it hard. After a second, the smoke from the exhaust pipe turns to blue and everyone begins clapping and cheering. Ghost stares in disbelief. "A boy," he whispers, looking down at me. I nod, smiling. "A fucking son?" I nod again, and he picks me up, spinning me around in delight. "You gave me a son."

"I did. How amazing am I?" I tease, wrapping my legs around his waist.

"Baby, you're perfect." I feel his erection at my entrance and smirk. "Let's disappear," he whispers against my mouth.

GHOST

I'm panting so hard, I think I'm gonna pass out. Lying beside Nelly, I try to get my breathing under control. "So, why is it okay to have sex now you know it's a boy?" she asks, running her fingers over the V-lines on my stomach.

"He's my kid, he can take it," I say, shrugging.

"A girl is just as strong," she argues. "She'll take after me."

I grin, throwing my leg over her and pulling her into my side. "You are very strong," he whispers, kissing my cheek. "The strongest woman I know."

"That's why I've made a decision," she tells me. "I'm going to see Hugo in prison."

"Not this again," I groan.

"I spoke to my therapist, and she thinks it will help give me closure."

"I'm sacking the therapist. She doesn't have a clue what she's talking about!"

I smile. "I have questions," she says, running her fingers through my hair.

"Don't give me that look," I mutter. "I'm not gonna be mentally bullied into this. I don't want you near him. I don't want you going to a prison, and who knows how it will affect you . . . and my son," I add, smiling as I say the word.

"Come with me. I'll ask my questions, and then we'll go."

"No, Nelly. I'm not agreeing to this. You're not seeing Hugo. End of."

I climb from the bed and head for the shower. I give in to a lot of things for Nelly, but not this. It's asking too much.

NELLY

"Ghost will kill me for this," complains Rosey.

"I'll deal with him," I say, pulling out my visitor's pass. I hand it to the man on the desk, and he ticks me off a list. We pass through the security checks and then we're ushered into a large room full of tables with chairs set either side. I spot Hugo instantly and feel sick. He looks smug as he watches us approach the table.

"Guilt got the better of you?" he asks bitterly. When I look confused, he smirks. "Fitting me up for a fucking murder I didn't commit," he hisses.

"I didn't," I mutter, wringing my fingers together.

"Bullshit. Funny they found a house key I had for your old place, with my name tag on it, at his office." I remember the day I gave Hugo that key because he laughed at the tacky name keyring I put on it. I also remember he gave it back and it had been in my underwear drawer at the clubhouse.

"I didn't set you up," I say, more firmly this time.

"What did your boyfriend do with the body? How did he hide it so fucking well?"

"Look, we came here to ask the questions, so shut the fuck up before I slit your throat in front of everyone," snaps Rosey.

"I thought you loved me once," I tell him, lowering my eyes to my wrist, where Ghost's name sits. I feel guilty and cover it over. "Why would you do that? Why didn't you stop him?"

"I thought you were drunk," he snaps. "How was I to know?"

"You've seen me drunk, Hugo, you know I wasn't drunk. Stop lying to me. It's over now, I just need the truth."

He leans closer. "The truth is, I'd have paid to see that kind of show, Nelly. Watching another man fuck you was better than fucking you myself."

I force down my tears. "So, it wasn't planned?"

"I might have told him you were an easy target, yeah. Your boyfriend broke my fingers," he growls. "Your parents wanted to leave you their half of the business and become silent partners. You! What would you know about running a business?"

"You arranged her attack so she wouldn't be in a fit state to take over?" snaps Rosey. "What the fuck is wrong with you?"

"I didn't even want the business," I mutter, frowning. "I wouldn't have agreed."

He leans back in his chair, shrugging. "What's done is done. I needed cash to offer your parents. I knew once they realised the place in France was bullshit, they'd stay put, and I wanted to make them an offer they wouldn't refuse. Why are you so hung up on it? Sex is sex."

Rosey's eyes almost pop out of her head. I place my hand on hers, a silent communication to stay calm. I lean over to the man at the next table, who I assume is with his wife and teenage daughter. He's huge and mean-looking. He scowls at me with furrowed brows. "Hey, I'm Nelly," I introduce myself.

"What the hell are you doing?" snaps Hugo.

"Signing your death sentence," I hiss. I turn my smile back to grizzly hulk. "I just thought you should know that this guy," I point to Hugo, "likes kids."

"Nelly!" yells Hugo.

"He's in here for raping teenage girls. More than one. He thinks he's untouchable and finds the whole thing amusing."

"Nelly, are you crazy?" Hugo yells. "They'll kill me." He grabs my arm in desperation, and a guard starts to make his way over.

I lean in close, grabbing his arm back and digging my nails into his skin. "You make me sick," I hiss into his ear. "I hope they rape you over and over so you can feel a fraction of the hurt and betrayal I felt when I learned that a man I loved, a man I thought loved me, watched my rape. All because you were scared I'd take over *my* family business. Rot in hell, you scumbag!"

The guard pulls us apart, and Rosey puts her arm around my shoulders and guides me towards the exit.

GHOST

I've not been this mad since . . . well, in a long time. When Nelly walks in with Rosey, laughing and full of excitement, I falter. It's been too long since I heard her laugh like that. She spots me and the smile fades. "Ghost," she mutters.

"Unless you're gonna follow that with a fucking apology, I don't wanna hear it," I growl. "I know exactly where you've been."

"I wasn't planning on lying about it," she says.

"And you," I hiss, glaring at Rosey, "always in the thick of the trouble."

She holds up her hands innocently. "Hey, I didn't want to go along with it. She made me."

"I asked you . . . no, I told you not to go and see Hugo. And you did it anyway. I hope you got the answers you so desperately needed," I snap.

Nelly walks towards me and gently places her hands on my chest. "I didn't get the answers I wanted," she admits. "He didn't apologise or tell me it was some horrible mistake, that he didn't mean to film it or say the things he said. But he told me he wanted me out the picture so I wouldn't feel able to take over from my parents in the business. He admitted to being pissed you broke his hand. And I just think he's messed in the head."

"So, she told another prisoner he's a paedophile. It was genius," cuts in Rosey, laughing.

I pinch the bridge of my nose. "You could have gotten hurt, Nelly. You're having my baby," I remind her. "You and my son are my priority. I should be able to trust you not to go ahead and put yourself in danger."

"I'm sorry," she says, and the look in her eyes tells me she's sincere. "I can close it now, that chapter is done. I'm ready to move forward and concentrate on you and the baby. No more dangerous missions, I promise."

"Yah know, the punishment for ignoring your old man's orders is huge," I warn, cocking an eyebrow.

She grins, running her hands over my chest. "Oh yeah?"

"Oh yeah," I repeat.

"Yuck, can you not do that here," groans Rosey. "Singleton right here!"

I bend swiftly, picking Nelly up. "I don't need telling twice," I say, heading for the stairs. "Don't expect to see her for the rest of the day," I throw over my shoulder. "I love you so hard," I tell her.

She smiles. "Like the most ever?"

I nod. "Like the most ever, baby."

THE END

Dice - The Perished Riders MC

Check out Dice's story here...

Chapter One
DICE

I clench my jaw, close my eyes, and take a slow, calming breath as I keep the dice tight in my grip. "Give me a number between one and six," I say, without opening my eyes.

"Please," whimpers the pathetic shitbag.

"One and six," I yell, opening my eyes and fixing him with a hard stare.

He sniffles. "Two," he mutters.

I give him a satisfied smile. "Two, good number." I loosen my grip on the pair of gold cubes in my palm and give them a light shake. Bringing my fist to my mouth, I blow for luck, something I've always done. I throw the dice, watching as they go up in the air, spinning slowly as they fall to the ground and clatter, rolling across the dirty concrete and crashing against the wall before landing neatly side by side. I take a step closer, peering at the black spots, and I wince. "Unlucky."

"No," he growls. "Please, I can sort this out. I know I can, but if you kill me, I can't."

I laugh. "Kill you? Who said anything about killing?" He glances nervously at the table where my bag is, my gun sitting neatly on top.

"Is it in my hand? You don't need to worry until it's in my hand. Now, let's talk."

"It's not as easy as you think to just bust her out of that place. It raises questions, and even if I did it, she'd never speak to you."

"She needs persuading."

"She's straitlaced, the kind of girl who's waiting for the right man."

I grit my teeth. "I *am* the right man—she just doesn't know it yet. The fact she's a good girl is the reason I need her." He frowns and it pisses me off. I'm sick of being looked at like that . . . like I'm fucking crazy. "I rolled a three. Wanna know what that means?" He shakes his head, and I grin. "It means I get to remove at least a third of your pinky."

"Come on, man," he cries, struggling against the restraints that hold him to the chair. "Please."

"I researched it, and you don't even need that finger. It does nothing." I shrug. "Unless you rest your mobile on it when you're flicking through social media." I stare at him for a second. "You don't look like you use social media, but I'll let you choose the finger. I'm easy." I go over to my bag and take out a knife. He struggles harder, this time making panicked pleas.

The door opens and Rosey bounces down the steps, humming one of her annoying tunes. She smiles sweetly, coming to a stop right beside my guy. "What'yah doin'?"

"None of your business. Get the fuck out."

"Maverick sent me to find you."

"And you just happened to know I'd be here?" I ask, arching a brow in her direction.

"I followed you. I was curious."

"You're obsessed," I mutter, taking the guy's hand to keep it steady, even though it's tied down at the wrist. He panics and begins yelling. Rosey rolls her eyes and slaps a hand over his mouth.

"I'm not obsessed. Maybe I'm bored?" She thinks about it and then nods. "Yeah, I think that's it. My mum used to say I was nosier when I got bored."

"Your mum was a whore. Did she even notice you?"

"Ouch, rude!" She watches as I bring the knife to his finger.

"You should tie it off," she says, and I pause.

"Huh?"

"You've got a white shirt on. You wanna tie the finger off, so the blood loss is less."

"No, I don't," I snap. "I know what I'm doing." I line the knife up just below the knuckle of his finger.

"Clearly, you have no idea. And why the little finger? What's the point?"

"Mind your business!" I growl.

"If it was me, I'd take the thumb."

I release the man's hand and sigh heavily. I can't concentrate with her going on in my ear. "Sorry?"

"The thumb," she repeats. "Think about it, there's so much you can't do without your thumb."

I notice the guy's gone quiet. He's passed out from the stress of the situation. I know how he feels—Rosey can cause a lot of stress. "Like?" I humour her.

"Wank," she states, nodding eagerly, and I almost laugh. Rosey slaps the guy, and he wakes with a start. "Hey," she says, smiling wide, "which hand do you use to masturbate?"

"I don't have time for this. Go away," I snap.

"What did you do to piss him off anyway?" she asks him.

"He wants me to persuade my friend to go out with him."

I groan, and Rosey laughs hard. "Are you shitting me?" she asks. "You wanna take a man's finger because you like his friend? Fuck, if she finds out, do you think she'll want anything to do with you?"

"She won't find out."

"He's gonna tell her," says Rosey.

"I won't," the guy promises.

"See, he won't," I say with a satisfied smile.

"Of course, he will. How long have you been friends?" Rosey directs her question his way.

"Forever," he admits.

"Forever! He's gonna tell her."

"Then I'll take more than his finger!"

"Take his thumb and his finger . . . definite wank stopper," she says, nodding.

"How about this," says the guy, and I'm thankful for the distraction from Rosey. "I'll bring her to your bar. Dice's, right?" he asks, and I nod. "I'll bring her tonight. You can charm her."

"She doesn't go to bars," I point out.

"What kind of woman doesn't go to bars?" asks Rosey, looking shocked.

"The good kind," I mutter.

"What do you want with a good girl?" she enquires, smirking.

Rosey wouldn't understand my need for pure and clean, my fascination with normal, everyday women who stick by rules and laws and have never seen bad things. "Okay, bring her tonight at eight. But I swear, if it doesn't work—"

"I'll slice off my own damn finger," he hisses as I cut the ropes from his wrists.

Once he's free, I hold out a hand for him to shake. He frowns, taking it cautiously. "No hard feelings, Cameron, you just got caught in the crossfire."

Rosey follows me back from the warehouse I own, a street away from the MC. All the brothers bought up the land surrounding the club, mainly cos we don't want neighbours rocking up and disturbing our life. And also because we always need buildings for storage or hiding things.

"I can help you with this woman," she says.

I laugh. "No chance. Stay away from her."

"Oooh, I'm intrigued. Who is the person getting you all hot under the collar?"

"None of your business. I mean it, Rosey. She's not from this world, so leave her alone."

"Then why d'yah want to get involved?" I ignore her, and she skips past me. "Fine, I'll show up and ask her myself."

I grab her arm and pull her back to me. She slams against my chest, and when she rears back, she's got her gun pointed to my head. "Try it, I dare you." She grins.

I smile. She'll never shoot me and get away with it. "I'm asking you nicely, Rosey. Stay away from Astraea."

"Astraea," she repeats. "Nice name." She tucks the gun away as I release her. "I'm serious, maybe I can put in a good word."

"No."

"You're no fun."

I'm agitated and I can't help it. She's late. We agreed on eight and it's almost twenty-past. "Everything okay, boss?" asks my bar manager, Stacy. I nod, not daring to speak because I know I'll snap. Finally, I spot Cameron entering the building. He looks nervous as fuck, and the second his eyes meet mine, he pales. Astraea isn't behind him. She's nowhere to be seen, and my fists curl into tight, angry balls. I keep my eyes fixed on him until he's standing before me.

"Let me explain."

"Where is she?" I ask through gritted teeth.

"Outside."

A sense of relief washes over me as I release the breath I'd been holding. "Okay. Well, bring her in."

"The thing is, she's not feeling well."

"Is she okay? Is she hurt?"

"No, nothing like that. I gave her a drink to help her relax, but it might have been too strong. She's never really had alcohol so—"

I don't wait for him to finish before I'm pushing people out of the way to get to her. Cameron is behind me, still trying to explain. When I set eyes on Astraea, hunched over by the wall with her head in her hands, I almost combust in an angry panic. "Why did you give her alcohol?" I growl, keeping my distance from her and holding Cameron back.

"She didn't want to leave with me, she was uptight and stressed. What was I meant to do? You made it clear what you'd do if I didn't get her here, so I did what I could."

"By getting her drunk without her knowledge?" I hiss. "Get over there and see if she's okay!" I shove him forward, and he stumbles over to Astraea while I linger behind.

"Hey, chica, how are you feeling?" he asks, gently placing his hand on her upper back. I itch to remove it.

"Oh, Cam, what did you give me in that drink?" she murmurs, not bothering to raise her head.

"It was a glass of Coke, Astraea. I'm not sure what's happening."

"I told you it tasted funny," she whispers. "I think it was off."

"Let's go inside and get you some water," suggests Cameron.

She shakes her head and immediately regrets it, groaning aloud. My cock twitches. "I can't go into a bar," she whispers.

"Of course, you can. The Lord won't strike you down for having a glass of water in a bar."

"No, but if my father found out, he'd—"

"He won't. Come on, Astraea, live a little."

"You can use my office," I say in a gruff voice. She looks up, letting her eyes trail the length of my body, and when they reach my face, her head is tipped so far back that she falls onto her arse with a humph.

She grabs Cameron by the arm and pulls him close. "Cam, there's a giant behind you," she whispers, flicking her eyes at me every so often.

"He's my friend," Cameron lies. "He owns this place. I told him you weren't feeling well."

"Where did you find a giant to befriend?" she asks, furrowing her brow. Man, she's cute.

Cameron laughs, hooking his arm under hers and tugging her to stand. She's wobbly, grabbing the wall for support. "I don't feel so good," she murmurs.

"Can you walk?" I ask. She shrugs, and I waste no time scooping her into my arms to carry her to my office. She giggles and the sound washes over me, making my heart beat double-time. Finally touching her after months of watching, longing to have this moment, makes me wanna never let her go. And it feels just as amazing as I knew it would.

ASTRAEA

I don't remember the last time I felt so bad. The room is spinning, and I feel sick. The kind of sickness you get when you've spun around in circles for too long or travelled over bumpy roads for miles. The giant marches through the bar with me in his arms like a ragdoll as people automatically move when they see him coming. He kicks open a door and we're in an office space. When the door closes, the noise from the club drowns away but leaves my ears ringing. At home, I'm not allowed to play music. My father hates it and much prefers silence.

The giant lays me on a worn-looking couch and steps back, staring down at me with interest. I've seen that look before in men's eyes, but it's wasted on me. I'm saving myself for my husband-to-be. Cameron comes into view, standing beside the giant. "Do you think she'll be okay?" he asks him.

"No thanks to you." The giant's voice is deep and growly, and I smile to myself. I like it.

"I overdid it," says Cameron, wincing.

"Yah think?" The giant produces a bottle of water and crouches beside me. "Here, Astraea, drink this. It'll help."

I take it with a shaky hand and half sit, all the time he remains beside me, close enough that I can smell his musky aftershave with a hint of cedarwood. I shake my head, clearing thoughts that have no place creeping in. It's not like I haven't met a handsome man before, but it's usually the kind introduced by my father.

I take a few sips and spill some down my chin. The giant moves swiftly, and I flinch. He frowns, slowing his hand as it approaches my face, and gently swipes away the water. The touch is so careful and soft, it feels barely there, but it's enough to send a thrill through my body, causing me to inhale in surprise. "I have to go," I whisper.

"Soon. You'll be in trouble if you go home like this," he replies, smiling. I can't help but return it. He's even more handsome when he isn't scowling.

"Maybe you should go and grab yourself a drink," says the giant, giving Cameron an annoyed scowl.

"He can't leave me," I protest.

He holds up a set of dice. "Pick a number," he whispers. "If I can roll it, he goes."

"Six," I reply, and his breath hitches. "It's my lucky number."

"Six it is," he murmurs, blowing on his hand before rolling them out onto my stomach. "Well, would you look at that. Cameron, ask for Stacy and tell her I sent you. Order whatever you like on the tab." He says it all with his eyes fixed on mine, and for some reason, I can't look away, even as Cameron leaves me alone with this stranger. The door opens and music fills the room as Cameron slips out, and once it's quiet again, the giant trails his fingers over my stomach and collects his dice. "How did you do that?" I ask.

"I didn't. The gods chose, Astraea," he says, adding a smirk.

"You know what my name means." I say it as a statement.

"The purest goddess. The virgin goddess of innocence, purity, and precision."

How does he know that? It's the first question most people ask when they meet me, because it's so unusual. "You know your history?"

"I was forced to go to god school as a kid. Bunch of nutjobs, if you ask me." He stands, turning away.

I push myself to sit farther, placing the bottle of water on the floor. "You don't believe in god?"

"Only my own."

"There's only one god," I say.

"Says who?" he asks, turning back to me. "Your father?"

My smile falters. "Do I know you?"

He takes a breath and releases it. "Is that your first drink?" I frown and glance at the water. "I mean the alcohol," he adds.

"I haven't drunk alcohol."

"Trust me, Six, you have. What you're feeling right now is drunk."

I shake my head, horrified. "No, I had a glass of Coke or two. There was no alcohol. I don't drink."

"Is that your choice or aren't you allowed?"

"I should leave." I stand, wobbling when the room spins. The giant's there in a flash, grabbing my hands to hold me up. "You look like a god," I whisper.

He smiles. "And you're a goddess, so that means . . ." He trails off, leaving the sentence open.

To continue, head here: https://mybook.to/Dice Bk5

A note from me to you

If you enjoyed Ghost, or any other books in the series, please share the love. Tell everyone, by leaving a review or rating on Amazon, Goodreads, or wherever else you find it. You can also follow me on social media. I'm literally everywhere, but here's my linktr.ee to make it easier.

https://linktr.ee/NicolaJaneUK

I'm a UK author, based in Nottinghamshire. I live with my husband of many years, our two teenage boys and our four little dogs. I write MC and Mafia romance with plenty of drama and chaos. I also love to read similar books. Before I became a full-time author, I was a teaching assistant working in a primary school.

If you'd like to follow my writing journey, join my readers group on Facebook, the link is above. You can also use that link if you're a book blogger, I'd love you to sign up to my team.

To follow all things Nicola Jane, head here: https://linktr.ee/NicolaJaneUK

Popular books by Niocola Jane

Riggs' Ruin https://mybook.to/RiggsRuin
Capturing Cree https://mybook.to/CapturingCree
Wrapped in Chains https://mybook.to/WrappedinChains
Saving Blu https://mybook.to/SavingBlu
Riggs' Saviour https://mybook.to/RiggsSaviour
Taming Blade https://mybook.to/TamingBlade
Misleading Lake https://mybook.to/MisleadingLake
Surviving Storm https://mybook.to/SurvivingStorm
Ravens Place https://mybook.to/RavensPlace
Playing Vinn https://mybook.to/PlayingVinn

Other books by Nicola Jane:

The Perished Riders MC
Maverick https://mybook.to/Maverick-Perished
Scar https://mybook.to/Scar-Perished
Grim https://mybook.to/Grim-Perished
Ghost https://mybook.to/GhostBk4
Dice https://mybook.to/DiceBk5

The Hammers MC (Splintered Hearts Series)
Cooper https://mybook.to/CooperSHS
Kain https://mybook.to/Kain
Tanner https://mybook.to/TannerSH

Printed in Great Britain
by Amazon